COURT OF RAVENS AND RUIN

THE SHADOW BOUND QUEEN

ELIZA RAINE

ELIZA RAINE

COURT OF RAVENS AND RUIN

THE SHADOW BOUND QUEEN
A BRIDES OF FAE AND MIST NOVEL

For everyone who never gives up.
For the love of Odin, you've got this.

GLOSSARY AND PRONUNCIATION GUIDE

Where possible names and places have been inspired by Norse language. Not all are listed here, but I have tried to include any with unclear pronunciation.

The World

Yggdrasil (EEG-dras-il) - the tree of life and common name for the world of the five Courts

Vald-staff (vawld—staf) - Staff that gives fae ability to use their magic

Rune-marked - human born with rune tattoos that match to one of the five courts, able to create vald-staffs for the fae

Gold-giver - rune-marked for the Gold Court
    Fire-forger - rune-marked for the Fire Court

Shadow-spinner - rune-marked for the Shadow Court

Water-winder - rune-marked for the Ice Court

Wood-worker - rune-marked for the Earth Court

Language Used in Yggdrasil

Veslingr (VEHS-ling-uhr) - An annoying coward

Valhalla (val-HAL-uh)- Heaven

Thrall (thrawl) – Slave

Heimskr (HEEM-skur) - Stupid

Names

Reyna (RAY-nuh)

Frima (FREE-ma)

Svangrior (svan-GREE-or)

Brynja (BRIN-yah)

Rangvald (RAHNG-vald)

CHAPTER I

"Have you found her?" My heart beat hard in my chest as I concentrated on the warrior before me.

The screams beyond him drowned out his first response. A Starving One stumbled toward the warrior, and fierce as I knew he was, he flinched. The creature was missing half its stomach and one arm, and mismatched skin tones made up the rest of its sewn-together body. Its open, gaping jaw was smeared with blood and its glassy lifeless eyes landed on the warrior's mighty axe.

Shadows spun around my staff briefly, before whirling toward the undead creature, absorbing it completely. An unearthly shriek faded to nothing.

"Have you found her?" I repeated, my voice granite.

"I believe we have, my Prince."

"We sail for her tonight. If anyone lays a finger on her, they die."

1

CHAPTER 2

"You cheated." The hulking, ale-stinking man before me reached out a hand as he grunted the words, his dirty fingers hovering over my black playing piece.

His eyes moved up to meet mine. They were red-rimmed and slightly glassy from all the ale, mead, and wine he'd consumed.

"Cheated? You are a sore loser, Skegin," I told him, batting his hand away.

"And you are a freak," he answered, casting a glance at my hair. Once, his words would have cowed me. Now they made me sit straighter, and a grin play on my lips. I lifted my hands, running them through my long copper hair.

"Rather a freak than a loser," I smiled at him.

He'd actually almost beaten me. For all his stench and disheveled appearance, he was one of the better players in Upper Krossa, the closest town to the Palace of the Gold Court. He was drunk, though. Something I was sure as Odin going to use to my advantage.

His eyes darkened at my taunt. "If I had hair that color, I'd cut it off," he snarled.

His own hair was a tangled mess of brown — the same shade of brown as all the other humans in *Yggdrasil*. I had never, ever seen another human with hair like my own.

"If I had no hair, then how would I show off all the braids I'm going to earn?"

He snorted at my reply. "You'll never earn braids. You must fight to earn braids." He banged a hand against his chest, sloshing ale from the tankard in his other hand over his already stained furs. The few men gathered around us in the alehouse slammed their own chests, cheering, then drank from their tankards.

I *could* fight, but I wasn't about to tell him that. And besides, to earn braids through fighting, you had to be honored by your clan. I had no clan.

I was owned by the palace.

"There are other ways to earn braids," I said. I needed to keep him talking, keep him distracted. If he spotted how easily he could defeat me, then I would be in trouble. I'd wagered far more than I could afford on this game.

This time, his eyes went to the gleaming golden rune etched into the skin on my wrist. "You are a thrall, just like me." His tone had turned harsher, the friendlier banter slipping away. "That rune doesn't make you any better than the rest of us humans."

3

It was true. The golden rune on my wrist didn't make me any better than other humans, but it did make me more valuable to our fae masters. I nodded slowly. "I'm better than you at this, though." I pointed casually to the board. "How about a new wager? I'll earn a braid before you will." He gave a big belly laugh and swigged from his drink.

"You will never earn a braid."

"Then take the wager." The tiniest flicker of doubt crossed his face. It was all I needed. "No?" I leaned forward, trying to ignore the pungent smell of livestock and ale. "You fear I would win, Skegin?"

The expression of doubt turned to anger, and I knew I had him where I wanted him. The rickety chair he was sitting on clattered backward as he stumbled to his feet. "You help the fae! You copper-haired witch, thinking you can leave the palace and treat us warriors like the shit on your boots! You're as bad as they are," he hissed.

I schooled my face, determined to keep any emotion from showing.

He was right though, my conscience screamed at me. *I enabled the greedy, cruel, brutal fae of the Gold Court to treat my whole race as slaves.*

I stayed sitting on my own chair and shrugged nonchalantly. "You are too stupid to win this game, and too cowardly to take my wager." My pulse quickened, knowing what the response would be. "To be honest, most small children are smarter than you. The actual shit on my boot might even give you a good challenge. Are you a *veslingr?*" Fury took his every feature as I used the ancient insult.

Unlike the greedy fae, the humans of the Gold Court still valued what Odin had instilled in the court centuries ago: valor, honor, and knowledge. If there was one way to goad a Gold Court human, it was to accuse them of being a coward, or of being stupid.

He kicked a foot out, sending the playing board flying toward the next table.

Victory surged through me. "That's a forfeit then," I said, standing quickly. I only just ducked the punch he threw at me. He had nearly a foot on me in height, and hadn't aimed well, so it was an easy dodge.

He gave a gurgly roar and tried to pull something from his leather belt, but his thick furs were blocking his clumsy scrabbling.

I took a risk and turned my back to him, to the wager-master sitting at the table behind us. I held my hand out.

"My winnings, please."

The younger, quieter man gave a coy look. "Well done, Reyna," he said. "It wasn't looking too good for you there." He knew exactly what I'd done. I flashed him a grin and he handed me a small pouch of jingling coins just as there was another shout from Skegin. I spun in time to see that he had extracted a small axe from his person and was aiming it at my head.

I gave him a small wave and a final smile, then ran.

Running may not have been the brave thing to do, but it was sure as Odin the smart thing.

I had no shield and was only wearing cotton clothes and workshop leather — I was in no position to defend myself. And besides, I had the coin I'd left the palace for.

I ducked past more uproarious drinkers and out of the doors to the alehouse, not pausing for a second before sprinting up the golden cobbled path toward the palace.

I knew he wouldn't follow me. He was too drunk, and he would find somebody else to fight with soon enough. It was the *Yggdrasil* way. Drink. Fight. Fuck. Repeat.

At least in the human towns, that was the way. The fae, they drank, they fought, they fucked. But fates, did they do it differently.

I glared at the glittering Gold Court palace as I raced toward it. The fae had built their home upon the central peak of the land that made up the whole of the court, so that it towered over the villages and towns below.

More than twenty towers made of pure gold rose majestically from the beautiful, tiered courtyards, wrapped in staircases shining with gilded carvings, and peppered with magnificent stained-glass windows reflecting the gleaming golden light of the rest of the Gold Court.

It should have been breath-taking.

Not to me.

It was the finest prison a girl could possibly despise. A gleaming noose around my neck, choking the life out of me.

The guards at the palace gates didn't bother stopping me as I ran past. My copper hair gave away who I was, and regular bribes meant they let me past reasonably often.

Hope burned in my gut. With the money in my new purse, I might finally have enough to get out of the Gold Court.

Enough to buy my freedom.

The same niggling doubts I always had crept into my mind in the form of Kara's voice. *"Reyna, you can't leave the Gold Court! You're rune-marked — every other court would try to kill you!"*

But when you've spent your life humiliated, used, and beaten by greedy, vicious fae, the prospect of death loses some of its bleakness.

It wasn't that I wanted to die, not at all.

But the dangers beyond the Gold Court had started to look different over the recent years, and things that had frightened me into obedience before, and still frightened my charge, Kara, no longer held the same terror. The Gold Court offered me protection, sure. But at what cost?

The stories about the Shadow Court still made my skin crawl, but surely I could find a place in one of the other three courts where I could be free?

My feet flew over the gleaming tiles of the enormous stairways carved into the tiered gardens, until I reached the level that housed some of the lesser fae courtiers, and the gold workshop. The golden spires reached up toward the sky above me, casting a shimmering glow like a cat's eye. Every step sent rays of light bouncing off one another, and I shielded my eyes from the gleaming gold walls and sent an angry look at the main gates of the palace two tiers higher, before ducking through the thrall's entrance. I slowed down to make my way as inconspicuously as possible through the gleaming hall. A few courtiers cast uninterested glances my way as I moved toward the concealed thrall quarters.

When I reached the workshop where I lived and worked, the guard frowned at me. She had smears of blue war paint on both cheeks and numerous braids in her brown hair, signifying that she was a human warrior of high respect. She was still a thrall though. A human slave.

"Where have you been?" Her barked words pissed me off instantly.

"Your husband's place."

Her spear thwacked me in the gut before I could react.

"You are pathetic, and a freak," she hissed at me.

"Uhuh. Better in bed than you though, according to your husband," I answered, trying to stay standing upright through the pain in my stomach.

Truth was, I was unlikely to be better in bed than anyone, based on the paltry and not particularly enjoyable experience I had in that area. Nor would I ever sleep with another woman's husband. But she didn't know that.

She stepped toward me, a nasty gleam in her eye. "You're wanted in the grand hall."

Icy cold trickled down my neck as a true fear took

me. "The grand hall?" I failed to hide my concern and her smile widened.

"Yes. Lord Orm is making his selection today, and guess what? You're one of the lucky final few."

My stomach flipped, and my pulse pounded in my ears.

Lhoris had warned me this may happen. My mentor had told me to keep my head down, attract no attention.

But apparently, I had failed.

There were a number of fates worse than death in *Yggdrasil*.

But an indefinitely long life as the bound concubine of the Gold Court's most cruel Lord? Other than being ripped apart and eaten by the Starved Ones, I couldn't think of any worse.

CHAPTER 3

I discreetly let out a long breath as I closed my eyes and counted to ten.

He might not choose me. He might not choose me.

There were five of us, lined up along the central carpet leading to the golden thrones at the end of the grand hall, framed by arched, gilded windows.

I glanced at the other four girls on the carpet with me. Two were much younger than me, and very pretty. The next woman was a lot older and absolutely beautiful. The last was my age and covered from head to foot in blue battle-paint and furs, any exposed skin mottled with white scars. She caught my eye, bared her teeth, then spat on the beautifully woven golden carpet beneath our feet.

My lips almost twitched into a defiant smile, but I caught myself in time. There was a loud crack, and her face contorted with pain. The thrall-master behind her snapped his whip.

10

"One day, I'll make you scream," he hissed.

She kept her lips clamped closed as one of the younger girls whimpered and looked nervously at her own thrall-master. The hulking man behind her gave her a leery grin but didn't move.

All five of us were thralls. Human slaves to the fae of the Gold Court. And all five of us had something one of the most powerful, and therefore wealthy, Lords of the Court wanted. I scanned the wrists of the other girls, my stomach sinking at the confirmation of what I already knew.

None of them were rune-marked. Which meant none of them were as valuable as I was.

The fae of *Yggdrasil* could only wield their loathsome magic with the help of vald-staffs. I looked down bitterly at the angular symbol burning bright gold on the inside of my wrist. The pattern was repeated larger between my shoulder blades. It marked me clearly to the fae as a *gold-giver*. A rare human who could craft magic staffs for the fae of the Gold Court.

A courtier swept past us with her escort, her fine embroidered dress and long braided blonde hair marking her as fae.

"Did you hear about the latest raids on the outer villages, my Lady?" the escort asked quietly. "Many human clans were dealt death."

The female's lips turned up, the tiny gold beads in her hair catching the light as she shook her head. "The stories of the Shadow Court's might are wildly exaggerated," she said. "They are but simple barbarians.

11

Anyway, a few human clans are no great loss." She raised her chin, gave me an appraising look, and moved past me to join the rest of the shallow, whispering crowd of courtiers who had turned up to line the halls and watch the Lord choose his new bound concubine.

I kept my snarl back, barely. In some ways, I hoped the vile fae female was right. I had grown up being told the horror stories of how the Shadow Court's telepathic powers were used to torture their slaves mentally, how they were brainwashed into killing their own loved ones, then forced to live in pitch-black dungeons filled with the decaying bodies of those they had murdered. Their specialty was fear and madness, and they were utterly remorseless.

I sent a brief prayer to Freya that any humans killed in the Shadow Court raids were spared such a trial and had been blessed with swift deaths.

A loud bang, signaling the doors to the hall being thrown open, interrupted my prayer.

Lord Orm strode along the carpet, casting his ice blue eyes over each of us. His grandeur was undeniable. He had skin almost as pale as bone, high cheekbones, and perfect, pointed ears. His clothes were much finer than that of the attending courtiers. Where they wore corsets and skirts, or fine leather warrior garb, he wore robes of white. Golden lace trimmed all the fabric, making him shimmer as he walked.

His thin, pale lips turned up in a delighted sneer when he saw the warrior woman.

"A human on her knees is a fine sight indeed." His

high-pitched voice rang through the room, and the simpering courtiers chuckled.

The warrior woman glared up at him, fury in her eyes. "I did not fight for Odin to be your fucking plaything," she spat.

Something dark flashed in Lord Orm's eyes. He tightened his grip on the staff in his hand, and a knot of helpless, guilty anger swished through my whole body. I recognized the staff. It had been the result of six months of my work.

"Playthings are for children," he said, voice low. "I am a fully grown male, which you would find out on entering my bedchamber." He gave her a sickening smile. "I think you may find that fighting your whole life will have prepared you well for what I have in store for my future concubine. I require a woman who is...robust."

Blessed Odin, I would do just about anything to avoid a binding to this male, but the warrior woman deserved this fate no more than I did.

Of the five courts of *Yggdrasil*, most would have believed that the Gold Court was the preferable place to live. It was the most powerful, the richest, the most beautiful.

But in reality, the Gold Court was fueled by nothing but greed. The principles instilled by the ancient god Odin had completely died out, knowledge no longer valuable compared with wealth and magic.

It was through the gold that their staffs gave them magic, and the lengths to which they would go to acquire it had turned them into monsters.

Beautiful, glittering, sadistic monsters.

Lord Orm was known to be one of the most twisted gold-fae. It was common knowledge in the palace that two of his previous concubines had died at his hand. Details of how had never surfaced, though the rumors were rife, and all of them made me feel sick.

"Strip. All of you." Lord Orm whirled around as he barked the command. Grinding my teeth, I reached to untie the leather band around my middle.

I was permitted to work in trousers and leather, whereas most female thralls in the Gold Court were forced to dress in skimpy shifts and thin skirts. My brown leather corset dropped to the floor around my feet when the ties came loose, and I moved my hands reluctantly to the belt at my waist. It was covered in small pouches that held the tools of my trade. Other than the gold I had to set into the staffs, of course. That was kept safe in the workshop, under fae guard.

I glanced either side of me as I slowly undid my belt, trying to stop my revulsion showing on my face.

Both the younger girls had already shed their thin garments, clearly used to being asked to disrobe. The older woman had her chin held high, and clear scars of childbirth showed on her stomach. The warrior woman had regained her footing, but her thrall-master was leering over her, pulling her fur-covered garb from her body as she hissed and clawed at him.

"You are making me weary," Lord Orm muttered.

"Some spirit in a female is preferable, but I fear I erred in asking you to take part in today's ceremony." He came to stop before her, and my fingers stilled on the waist of my trousers.

"She will do as you command, my Lord," grunted her thrall-master.

Lord Orm cocked his beautiful head. "I'm not sure that she will. Ever."

She moved quickly, making to stamp on his foot, close as he was to her.

His fae speed was no match for her fierce spirit. He side-stepped so fast he was almost a blur. The gold entwined throughout his staff glowed briefly before he bought it crashing into the side of her head.

His fae strength was as instantly apparent as his speed had been.

The woman's body dropped to the floor, lifeless. I turned my head quickly to stop myself staring at the gaping hole in the side of her skull. Fear crawled icily through my veins, my breakfast threatening to rise up my throat.

Lord Orm sighed, tilting his pale head. "Odin's raven, I didn't mean to hit her that hard," he muttered. "No matter, she was unsuitable. I shall reimburse you for your lost thrall. Please see my purse-keeper on your way out."

Still unwilling to look, I heard the thrall-master, now void of his thrall, grunt. "Thank you, my Lord." Heavy footsteps thumped through the room as he left the hall.

"And then there were four," sang the Lord. "Why are

you still dressed?" He moved into my line of vision, and I couldn't help meeting his eyes. I stilled the tremble in my fingers and resumed removing my trousers.

I moved my gaze to his staff, trying to focus on it, to calm my fear. Held in the end of the metal shaft was a gently glinting orb, the size of an eye. Around it was a ring, also made from gold, and flowing from the ring were twenty golden leaves. I had crafted every one painstakingly, and individually. No two staffs could be the same, and the stronger the design, the stronger the staff.

This staff has just caused the death of a woman. It's hardly going to calm you down, Reyna.

The tinge of red against the gleaming gold made the tremble threaten to return as I crouched, sliding my trousers down my legs.

"Too slow." Lord Orm lifted his staff as I straightened. A beam of bright light shone from the top, moving over my body like a torch. Everywhere the light touched, the moss-green fabric of my shirt burned away. The garment fell in tattered ribbons around my feet, leaving me standing in nothing but my cotton knickers.

In all my years as a thrall, my whole damned life in fact, I had never felt so vulnerable. I'd been made to strip many times. I had been beaten and thrashed many times. But I was too precious to be soiled. My status as a rune-marked had provided me a degree of safety. At least, it had kept me in control of my own body. The energy required to use my craft was massive, so my mind and body must be alert and ready for work, always. Nothing

16

was more valuable to the Gold Court fae than their staffs, and therefore the rune-marked who could forge them.

Now though, my thrall-master had no say. Lord Orm was not a male to be told no.

Slowly, he reached out a hand and placed it on my shoulder. My skin crawled at his touch, but I let him turn me around. He paused when my back was to him, and I felt him press a cool finger to the rune on my spine.

"A *gold-giver*," he murmured. "Useful, to have a bound female that, in addition to servicing my needs, could also keep my staff in pristine condition."

I sucked in air, trying to keep calm.

He won't hurt me. Not here, not today. I'm worth too much to him.

"I could even rent you out to my friends. But who ever saw a human with hair this color?" He turned me back to face him and lifted a handful of my hair to wave it in front of my eyes.

Lord Orm's lips pulled back in distaste as he dropped the clump of hair. "That would have to change." A flash of defiance almost showed on my face, and I felt my lips part in protest.

For two decades, my hair had caused me nothing but grief. It made me different, made me stand out. It had made me a target, even within the enslaved human community. But my treatment by those around me had made me stronger than the other humans. It had forced me to stand up for myself, to constantly be one step ahead. My hair had become my armor.

"You have something to say on the matter, little *gold-*

giver?" Lord Orm's words were a whisper, almost seductive. Gooseflesh rose on my arms when the gold in his staff glowed.

An image swam through my head, hazy but impossible to dispel.

It was of me, tied to a bed covered in milk-white sheets, with four golden posts at each corner. I was face down, naked, the rune on my back criss-crossed with red welts from the whip.

"Nothing, my Lord," I forced myself to say as his vision sapped my strength. My voice was small and weak. I hated it. Despised it. Despised myself for submitting.

Lord Orm stared at me a long moment as I tried to force the image out of my head.

"This one!" he announced with a flourish, lifting his staff and casting it toward me.

He hadn't even looked at the others.

Blood pounded in my ears, and black dots flickered across my vision as the magical one of me on the bed faded.

The hope that had burned behind my fear fled as reality punched me in the gut.

I would become the cruel fae's bound concubine.

Which meant the life of servitude I had lived so far would look like a fucking paradise.

CHAPTER 4

"You're uncharacteristically quiet," sneered the guard when we were beyond the gates of the grand hall and in the lower echelons of the palace.

"Fuck you," I hissed without turning to her, quickening my steps along the golden corridors. The beauty of the intricate paintings, marble carvings, and glittering gemstones were lost on me entirely. My mind was moving at a pace I could barely keep up with, my stomach still churning as I held the pathetic blanket I'd been given around my shoulders, trying to conceal my naked body.

She chuckled. "Ah. There it is. The true nature of the copper-haired brat. Lord Orm will enjoy you and your barbed tongue, I'm sure."

For a second, my steps slowed, as I almost turned and landed my fist in the middle of the smug expression I knew she would be wearing.

But I forced my legs to keep moving. Getting the lash for hitting my guard would take too much time. Time I no longer had.

I kept my lips shut tight as we made our way back to the workshop. I shared the space with four other *gold-givers* who had been found and enslaved to the palace. Two of whom I loved dearly, but the other two? They could sail straight to *Hel* for all I cared. My copper hair had been all the reason they needed to treat me like dirt for years.

"Reyna!" Kara leaped up from her workbench and raced over to me as soon as I entered the workshop. The young girl's face fell when she saw me. Her eyes flicked to the blanket around me, then back to mine.

"He's coming to get you tomorrow morning. Clean up," the guard barked, then turned and left, locking the heavy door behind her.

"Oh no. Oh no, no, no," Kara whispered, her eyes wide and round. "We heard you got called for consideration for Lord Orm. Please tell me he didn't choose you?"

I took a deep breath. "He chose me."

She bit down on her lip, making herself look even younger than she was. "Maybe... Maybe he won't be cruel to you?"

"He killed a woman. In front of everyone. One of the women brought for consideration."

Her brown eyes widened further. "Killed her? Why?"

"She tried to stamp on his foot."

"Precisely the reason I schooled you in being meek around powerful fae." The deep voice belonged to Lhoris, my mentor. I turned to him as he lumbered toward me. His age and experience in crafting vald-staffs meant he was allowed a single braid in his huge beard. He had fought valiantly for his clan before he was recognized and enslaved as a rune-marked, so a blue smear of war paint permanently adorned the cheek under his left eye.

I nodded at him. "I did as you told me. I bit my tongue. I even took my damned clothes off without a word."

One of his eyebrows twitched, and anger flitted through his wise eyes. "I am proud of you, Reyna." He paused, shifting a razor-sharp sculpting blade from one hand to the other. "And... I am sorry."

I fixed my eyes on his. "Don't be. I'm leaving, Lhoris."

I saw no surprise on his face. Only sorrow.

Kara gripped my arm. "You can't leave!"

"Well, I'm sure as Odin not being bound to Lord Orm."

"But you're a *gold-giver*!" I looked at my young protégé, my emotions churning. I had to look strong for her. I had to hide how I really felt about abandoning her to this twisted fucking Court. I had to make her think I would be safe.

"I will find a way to hide my rune-marks," I lied. There was no way the marks could be hidden. And even if they could, my copper hair drew attention like a flame to the moths.

"No, no, Reyna! The other Courts will find you. The raids are constant now! You would be running straight to your death."

Her fears were not unfounded. The runes that marked me as valuable to the Gold Court also marked me for death in any of the other four Courts.

The wars between the fae raged long and deadly, and the quickest way to cripple an enemy court was to remove their magic. The highest prize besides killing an actual fae member of the Court was killing one of the rune-marked they relied on for their staffs.

Kara shuddered and whispered, "What if the Shadow Court found you?"

Which was the only reason I hadn't left already.

If a *gold-giver* was found by Ice, Fire or Earth Courts, then they would be killed on the spot, then their body would be dragged back to their palace for a reward to be claimed. But if a member of the Shadow Court found a *gold-giver*?

The Queen of the Shadow Court, along with her stepson, was supposed to be the most cruel and vicious of all the living fae, and the war between Gold and Shadow was the oldest and most brutal of all the feuds. Odin help any gold-giver the Shadow Court got their hands on.

"I'll stay in the Gold Court. Live with the humans in the lower villages," I told Kara. Another lie. Lord Orm was too powerful to hide from in his own Court. Kara was looking at me, a mix of doubt and fear on her face. "Or the Earth Court," I said cheerfully. "They aren't known for exceptional violence."

She gave me a look. "They burn thralls every full moon," she said, fisting her hands on her hips. "And they get raided by the Shadow Court more than any others!"

Her voice wobbled. "The Shadow Court make you kill your own friends," she whispered. "And I heard they feed humans to the Starving Ones."

I swallowed hard. Would that be worse than being bound to Lord Orm? Killing my own or being eaten alive, versus a life in servitude to that greedy, sadistic fae?

An image of the warrior woman's crushed skull swam through my head. She had died quickly. She was honorable, and a warrior, so she would go straight to Valhalla.

But Lord Orm wouldn't kill me. I was too valuable. And as one bound to the fae, I would share his much-extended lifespan. An eternity enduring whatever he deemed his concubine deserved. My stomach knotted.

"You should dress," Lhoris said, glancing between me and Kara's tear-filling eyes. "And then, if you have time, I could do with your help with finishing a staff. Once it is complete, we can discuss the practicalities of you escaping the palace."

I nodded at him, feeling a swell of gratitude both for the offer of help, and his practical tone. My mind was swimming with fear and confusion, and I didn't think I was hiding very well from Kara. I turned back to the girl. "Kara, can you prepare me half an ounce of gold, please?"

She nodded, then scurried toward the forge.

The rune-marked wing was essentially one giant workshop, with four rooms off it that housed two bunkrooms, a toilet and tub, and a larder. The workshop was split down the middle by a massive stone trough filled with molten brimstone, traded at a high price from the Fire Court. Lining the outer walls were our benches, well-lit by large windows that let in the sparkling light of the Gold Court.

I glared at the view. More than half the humans who lived in the towns below were thralls to the fae.

They said humans were too barbaric to be allowed to rule themselves. They said that's how the Starving Ones came into being. I shuddered. The ancient mythical clan were said to have become so hungry and desperate that they turned on each other. *Ate* each other. And the gods punished them with the intensity such an abhorrent act deserved.

But that didn't explain why the fae hadn't been able to put an end to their miserable existence.

I forced down the familiar feeling that came whenever I thought about the Starving Ones and moved quickly to the bunkroom I shared with Kara and the other female gold-giver. To my relief, the room was empty. I dressed quickly in a black shirt, brown leather corset and black breeches and swapped the slippers I'd been made to wear in the grand hall for my leather boots.

"Kara's right," Lhoris said when I exited the bunkroom and found him waiting for me.

"About which part?"

"If the Shadow Court find you, they'll kill you instantly." He glanced over his shoulder at me. "Or worse."

"I won't be going anywhere near the Shadow Court. I'll hide in the Earth Court. I've always wondered how they make staffs from wood."

"Reyna, they'll kill you too, the second they see your rune-mark. The other courts are—."

I finished his sentence for him, so often had I heard him say the words. "Cutting the head off the golden snake. I know, Lhoris." He stared at me, and I laid my hand on his arm. "What would you do, in my position?"

Pain turned to anger in his dark eyes. He must have made a fearsome warrior. Valhalla would welcome him for certain. "I would not become the toy of that monster."

I shrugged, trying to keep my growing panic at bay. "Exactly. It's the monsters within, or the monsters without. Only, this one already knows where to find me."

He nodded, resignation making his jaw tight. "Run."

"Run," I repeated on a breath.

Saying the word aloud helped. *This is happening, Reyna. You're really running.*

Freedom. Just so long as I spent my likely short life in hiding.

"Do you really need my help finishing a staff? Or did you just wish to speak privately?"

He grunted and turned back to his bench. "You are better at feathers than I am," he said. "And if you are really leaving, then you might want to use your craft one more time." I followed him, trying to keep my face from showing my sadness.

I would miss him fiercely. And Kara. They were the only thing like family I had ever known.

And I would fear for them too. Lhoris could fight his own way to his destiny, but Kara? She was pretty, and easily cowed. A dangerous combination in a world where one was surrounded by gilded sharks. I had made some progress with her confidence over the two years she had been under my tutelage, but she could still so easily be taken advantage of.

Lhoris interrupted my thoughts once more as I sat down at his bench, leaning his bulk over my shoulder. He pointed to an intricate gem-set arch at the end of a gleaming staff laid across the worktop.

"You see this halo section, over the gem?"

"Yes."

"She wants feathers all along both sides."

"No problem."

Kara appeared beside me, and her small hand shot out, a tiny ball of shining molten gold in the middle of her gloved palm.

"Thank you."

"Can I watch?" she asked me. "As... as it might be the last time..." She trailed off, eyes filling again.

"Of course you can."

I took some forceps and lifted the gold from her hands. The rune on my wrist heated, glowing brightly — the signal that I could touch the heated gold.

None of us knew how or why, but those born rune-marked had access to a vein of magic within the gold itself, and it overpowered the senses like a drug.

As soon as I picked up the metal, my vision changed. A tinge of warm yellow colored everything, and lines of shimmering, liquid magic swirled around the nugget of gold. As they swirled, I could see little runes in the ripples, sparkling as though they were made of glitter. With my other hand, I moved the arch I was supposed to decorate toward me. The runes changed, the magical streams flowing from the nugget to the staff.

It was a language I had never been taught, but innately understood. The more I used my ability, the more runes I could read. They told me where to put my fingers, how to use my finer tools, exactly where to join the precious metal. They showed me the steps to a dance nobody could ever perform unaided.

I fell into the trance, my fingers moving practically of their own accord, following the playful, sparkling instructions of the tiny magical golden runes. I never knew how much time passed when I was working, never needed to stop for a break or for refreshment. It was an escape from the world entirely.

At least as long as I was doing it. Once the work was over.... That was different.

When I had twenty tiny, perfectly detailed feathers attached in a flowing line over the arc, the gold-vision fell away, the cold, harsh tones of real life slamming back into place before my eyes.

Exhaustion seeped through me, bone deep. "How is

that?" I asked Lhoris, pushing the stool back. I knew what was coming next, and I wanted to be alone.

"Perfect," he said, leaning in to examine them. Kara leaned in too, eyes darting over the details of the staff. "Rest, and then we will make plans."

I nodded and made my way quickly to the bunkroom. The first wave of darkness hit me as I reached my bed. I closed my eyes as I sat down and drew a breath. There were usually three or four waves. The first was always the easiest. Shadows and dankness, a strong sense of unease.

I gripped the hay-stuffed mattress as the second wave hit. Unease changed to fear. Sounds I had never heard in real life before filtered through my ears, an unearthly screeching laugh. I saw nothing but darkness, interspersed with flashes of deep red.

I had always had the dark visions after working with gold, ever since I was a child. When I had been brought to the palace, and Lhoris had taken me under his wing, it had taken me months to build up the courage to ask him if he experienced them too.

He had told me that he didn't and to keep them to myself.

The third wave reached me, always starting with a splitting scream, followed by the awful screeching laugh. The shadows cleared a little, enough for me to see figures moving awkwardly, figures that were not right somehow. The smell of blood filled my nostrils.

You're in your room, Reyna. There's no blood here. It's not real.

The smell always got me the worst. I didn't understand how a vision could carry a smell.

A face started to come into view on my left, and fear crawled up my chest. The vision faded.

"Please let it only be three today," I whispered aloud.

I'd never told anyone but Lhoris about the visions, and I hadn't even told him the full truth.

I had never told him what I saw in the less frequent fourth vision.

I couldn't.

I knew what I was seeing, but I didn't know how it could be possible. I didn't *want* to know.

Bile rose in my throat as a feeling of pure terror washed over me. "Fuck," I swore, then blackness took my eyes. The face moved clearly into view, a maniacal grin on the blood-stained maw. She had once been human, but it was clear she wasn't any longer. Parts of her cheek and her ear were gone, ragged edges on the torn skin. Her eyes were completely black, and she had no lips. A gnarled hand moved toward me, three fingers missing.

I hissed out a desperate curse, and the vision cleared. Panting, I dropped back onto the bed. Sweat seeped through my shirt.

It didn't matter how many times I saw the Starved Ones, it always terrified me like it was the first.

CHAPTER 5

"So, you need to get past the guards on our door, the guards on this floor of the palace, the guards at the gates to the palace, and then...all the way to the tree, without being recognized or stopped?"

Kara was staring at me like I'd lost any sense I might once have possessed. And I couldn't really blame her. I rubbed a hand across my face.

"What if I become Lord Orm's concubine and find a way to cut his balls off instead?" I offered.

Kara blushed and Lhoris snorted a laugh. "Prick would deserve it," he grunted.

"I'd be doing all females a favor." I was trying to keep the banter up, but the truth was that my head was still spinning. I was facing impossibilities on all sides. The impossibility of being bound sexually to a male like Lord Orm versus the impossibility of surviving outside of the Gold Court's protection. Not to mention, the impossibility of escaping the Gold Court.

"The guard really said he was coming for you tomorrow?" asked Kara.

"Yes. Tomorrow. We only have tonight."

We were sitting around a small table in the larder room. Fortunately, there had been no sign of our fellow *gold-givers*. They must have been on private jobs. It often took weeks to do repair work, and it was not uncommon for the *gold-givers* to stay in the fae quarters during the jobs. Most rune-marked needed massive amounts of rest once they had worked. I had never found that to be the case, but I chose to keep that to myself. It gave me a chance to be on my own when the visions came.

"I'll miss you." Kara's voice was tiny. I felt my face heat, my usual reaction to emotion. Tears did not fall easily for me, but I felt my emotions no less than those who cried. For some reason, my body reacted with flushed anger in place of salty tears.

"If it were not so dangerous, I would take you with me in a heartbeat." I told her. I'd never known any family other Kara and Lhoris. My resolve wavered as I looked between them. Was the risk worth it?

Was the loss of the only two people in the world who loved me worth it?

Another unexpected internal battle had arisen within in me. Every time I thought of never working with gold again, a flash of fear burned me. Was I addicted to the work, like a warrior to ale, or peasants to the poppy? The sparkling golden runes were a part of me. Perhaps I needed them.

Lord Orm is one of the Queen's favorites. He might let me

continue to work in the palace with Lhoris and Kara, and the gold.

At the thought of the Lord though, the vision he'd sent of me naked and tied to the bed took over my mind. Revulsion rushed through my veins at what he might do to my body, and I hurried to stem my spiraling thoughts.

No. I would rather risk death than let Lord Orm do whatever he wished to me, for an interminably long time.

The light streaming in through the large windows dimmed and all three of us froze.

The light *never* dimmed in the Gold Court.

"What's happening?" whispered Kara.

"Hush," hissed Lhoris.

We all strained our ears, listening, barely breathing.

The distant sound of metal clashing reached me, and I looked at Lhoris. He gave a tiny nod, and I leaped to my feet, tugging Kara up.

"You hide in the larder cupboard, and you do not come out." I pulled her toward the wooden towers of cupboards. Her face was a mask of panic.

"What's happening?"

"I don't know. Tell me you understand me."

She nodded, face pale. "Don't come out of the cupboard."

"Good." I knelt, pulling rolls of dried meat and sacks of vegetables out of one of the lower cupboards and stuffing it all hastily into another. "There, there should be space. Get in."

She threw her arms around me, her slight body trembling. "I don't want you to leave."

I tightened my own around her, heart pounding. "I know. I've loved working with you, Kara. You're going to be the most amazing *gold-giver* ever, and don't let anyone give you any ideas otherwise. You're in charge of you, nobody else. Now, hide." I placed a kiss on the top of her head, so light I wasn't even sure she was aware of it. She released me, and ducked down, folding herself into the cupboard. Her cheeks were streaked with tears.

"Stay silent until Lhoris comes for you."

I whirled before the sight of her terrified face could compel me to stay with her, breaking into a run.

Lhoris was at his bench. Anything that could be used as a weapon was gathered before him: heavy hammers, sharp scalpels, and his own hard-earned battle-axe.

"What's happening?" I panted as I reached him. His face was grave. The sounds of swords and spears clashing was louder now, some very human sounding shouts audible too.

"Only one thing can make the light of the Gold Court dim." Fear coiled in my gut. I knew what he was going to say.

"The Queen's sister?"

He nodded grimly. "Or her son, the Prince of the Shadow Court."

∾

I made to grab for the smelting hammer on his work bench, but he reached out a hand and stopped me, grabbing my wrist.

"This is your chance."

"To what, die? If the Shadow Court are raiding the palace, then things have escalated between the Queens."

"Escape, Reyna. If there was ever a distraction that could be taken advantage of, then this is it."

I stared at him, recognizing the determination in his eyes. "Are you going too?" I whispered.

A pang of longing sparked in the deep brown, but he shook his head. "I'll stay. For Kara."

Relief washed over me. She would be safe with him. "Thank you."

He gave a grunt, then spoke. "You should take this." He held up the staff I'd finished for him earlier, with the twenty feathers.

"What? No! You would be thrashed to within an inch of your life!"

His shoulders squared. "It would be worth it, for you to have such a valuable bartering tool on your journey. And besides, I believe enough chaos has struck the palace that I will be able to plead ignorance to its disappearance."

I only hesitated a second longer. "Thank you." I closed my hand around the staff. "Again."

"Thank me by making something of your life that I never could, child." The honest emotion in his face made my own burn. "Now, get your bag. This is it, Reyna."

I sprinted to my bunkroom. I threw my meager

belongings in a shouldersack, but took care to wrap the staff in the only thick fur I owned. The painted metal handles of all the staffs we made were designed to collapse in on themselves, so that they could be stored, transported, or in this case, hidden, easily. I could feel its weight though, when I donned the bag.

"I'm ready," I said, running back into the workshop. I tried not to feel alarmed by how much darker the sky outside had become. The glittering, reflective golden light had never been absent from the workshop, in all the time I had lived there.

There was a loud thump from the locked doors, and Lhoris swiped up a razor-sharp scalpel, raising it alongside his axe.

Apprehension skittered through me as I moved to his side, picking up the hammer.

"Be ready," he murmured, as another thump sounded, even louder.

I opened my mouth to reply, but my words faltered at the cold that shrouded me suddenly.

Something was wrong.

Fear that ran too deep to be attributed to the fight-ready battle tension I'd been experiencing a minute ago was crippling my thoughts.

Shadows.

There were shadows moving under the door, like lethal black smoke.

Slowly, painfully slowly, the shadows tightened, forming long black snakes.

My fingers trembled around the handle of the hammer.

I'd heard of the shadow snakes.

They said the snakes were the last thing any of his enemies saw, before they lost their sanity completely. There was only one fae in all of *Yggdrasil* who could conjure them.

The Shadow Court Prince.

Fear, not just for myself and my friends but for what I might be forced to do to them, made me want to cry out, or even hide with Kara.

You're stronger than this, Reyna, I half shouted at myself in my mind. *This is your chance to escape!*

But none of this was what I had expected.

I had expected the human clans who fought for the Shadow Court. I had expected blood-thirsty warriors wielding axes and spears, too intent on killing each other to notice my escape. I had expected Lhoris and his axe to stay in the workshop and defend Kara if any of those warriors strayed too far from their fight.

I had been wrong.

The doors creaked, then burst open, revealing a figure seven feet tall and shrouded in black.

The fight had come to us, and it was no human warrior.

"Good evening, little *gold-givers*," said the Prince of the Shadow Court, stepping out of the shadows and into the room.

CHAPTER 6

For a beat or two, I couldn't catch my breath. Icy fear doused me from head to foot, and numbness took my fingers.

Shadows pushed at my mind, edging my vision, making my thoughts cloud.

Was this how it started? Was he about to take over my mind and force me to kill Lhoris? The huge man beside me hefted his axe with a snarl and the Prince chuckled from beneath his deep hooded cloak.

Was he about to make Lhoris kill me?

Paranoia and magic-induced fear was paralyzing me. *For the love of Odin, get a grip on yourself, Reyna!*

My fingers finally moved, tightening on the hammer handle.

Slowly, the Prince lifted his staff. Shadows swirled gently from the end of it. The staffs I made were topped with huge gemstones, or if the owner was very wealthy, orbs of gold, but this staff had a skull. A black skull, barbed with spikes, with a halo of twisted thorns arching protectively over it.

The shadows tightened into ribbons, then rushed toward the Prince's head, pushing his hood back.

I sucked in a breath and did everything I could to hold my ground.

He was wearing a mask that matched his staff. The black skull covered his own, save for the gaps large enough to see his bright grey eyes through. His black shadow-fae hair was braided away from his face at the top, but fell over his shoulders. The beads in his braids were skulls too. His body was wrapped in black furs and leathers, and everywhere my eyes skimmed I could see the gleam of weapons.

"My Prince!" roared a voice from beyond the doors he had just broken through.

The shadows whirled from where they were circling his neck, flying toward the heavy doors and slamming them closed.

Odin help me, he was strong. I was around magical fae regularly, and whilst gold-fae magic was less visceral and violent than shadow-fae magic, few of the fae I knew could control objects like he just had.

"You will come with me. Now." His voice was deep and rich, and I couldn't tell if the command was laced with magical compulsion or if he just had lethal authority.

What I was certain of though, was that the command had been aimed at me.

I tried to force my racing thoughts to slow enough to

think straight.

Lhoris stepped forward. "We are going nowhere."

Where the fuck were the guards? The gold-fae had a chance at repelling him, but us? We had absolutely none.

The numbness seeped from my limbs and adrenaline began surging through my body in its place. I gripped the hammer, lifting it higher. If I was going down, I was going down fighting.

The Prince took a step toward us. "I do not need you. Just her."

Me? If he was here to round up and kill rune-marked, why didn't he want Lhoris too? My mentor was more skilled than I was, and a greater asset to the Gold Court.

"I will defend her to the death," barked Lhoris.

The Prince cocked his head. "You are lovers?" The deep, rich tone had turned to a hiss.

Lhoris growled. "She is family. I will die before you take her."

All the emotion that had built up over the last few hours and all the work I had done in convincing myself I could leave the two people who loved me, blazed hot in my chest. And for me, emotion meant anger.

Lhoris would die to protect me.

And I, he.

"We're going nowhere," I said, finally finding my voice. "The gold-fae will be here any second."

The Prince laughed softly. "Your gold-fae are pathetic, greedy peacocks. They will defend their riches before they come anywhere near you."

He was probably right, but I lifted my chin, and

shifted the hammer. His shadows swirled around him, and light blazed in his eyes. "You are not alone here."

A band of terror tightened around my ribs at his soft words. "We are."

He shook his head slowly. "No." With a flick of his staff the shadows whooshed toward the larder.

Every instinct in me wanted to race them there, but that would give Kara away. "There is nobody else here," I repeated, louder.

"I can smell her fear."

A sickening feeling joined the tight band.

He knew.

There was a scream from the larder, and with a piercing glance at me, he swept past us.

"Lhoris, what the fuck do we do?" I hissed.

His face was grimly set. "We fight."

The *Yggdrasil* way.

But we couldn't win. I was no coward, but I was no fool either.

"Reyna!" Kara ran into the room from the larder, the shadows whipping at her leather apron as she rushed toward me. I held out my free hand, gathering her into my side. The shadows skimmed my clothes, and a rush of cold tricked across my skin.

I looked at the Prince, who was staring into the now empty larder. The mask prevented me even guessing at his thoughts, but something had his attention.

Without hesitating, I moved, pulling Kara with me. I had only gotten six paces toward the doors before they burst open again.

A warrior ran into the room. Black war paint covered his skin, and his black braided hair marked him as shadow-fae. An axe in his hand was crimson with blood.

"Time to leave, my Prince," he called.

The Prince whirled. "All of you, then," he said.

"No! If it's me you want, just take me."

His eyes found mine and he gestured at Lhoris. "This man is determined to make my life difficult, and I do not have time to kill him now. I would rather do so at my leisure, in my own Court."

"Then leave the girl. She's just a child."

"No." He moved toward the warrior, and his shadows spun around us. "If you do not follow me without a fight, I will slit her throat. If you try to run, I will turn her body inside-out."

A guttural sound escaped my throat, causing him to pause and look over his shoulder at me. "You have three seconds to make your choice."

I knew with all the certainty in the world that he was capable of his threat. I looked from his black skull mask to the warrior's blood-soaked axe.

"Reyna?" Kara whispered, terror in her voice.

"We go without a fight," growled Lhoris, before I could utter the same words.

We stood no chance of winning a fight. But I wasn't giving up on running.

I hugged Kara to me. "Do not leave my side, you hear?" She nodded, her trembling arm tightening around me.

Beyond the doors to our workshop, the tiled floor was littered with bodies. They wore both gold and black armor, Gold and Shadow Court humans alike, dead for their cause. I could see no fae victims though. My heart skipped in my chest as we were pushed toward the thrall's stairs. There on the ground, her lifeless eyes staring at the tiles, was the guard I'd so desperately wanted to punch just earlier that day.

As we started down the spiral staircase another two warriors joined us, out of breath and covered in blood.

"The battles rage on the upper levels, my Prince. We need to make haste, but we should not be hindered once out of the palace," the female warrior said.

The sounds of fighting died away, and when we exited the seemingly eternal stone staircase into the entrance hall at the bottom level of the palace, there was indeed no battle raging. Just more bodies of the fallen.

They will feast in Valhalla, I told myself as the tang of blood filled my nostrils.

They died fighting. Honorably.

Their cause wasn't honorable though. Anger bubbled through me as we passed more dead slaves as we moved through the glittering courtyards, and at the grand palace gates. Their cause was nothing but fae greed.

The golden cobbled path beyond the palace gates was eerily quiet. One lone white stallion galloped past us, riderless, disappearing into the vast copse of yew trees on our right.

Jealousy of the animal's freedom coursed through me, and I tried to work out any way of following the horse.

But the three warriors that had joined the Shadow Court Prince had closed in around us, walking in formation. There was no chance of running yet.

The Prince was in the lead, his cloaked back to us and shadows still whirling gently around the top of his staff. He moved with lethal grace, and he'd not said a word since entering the workshop.

Why did he want me?

The question was burning to be asked, drowning out most other thoughts in my head.

I could understand the Shadow Court raiding the palace and killing *gold-givers*. But we should already be dead. All three of us. Why the fates had he taken us captive? *Why the fates had he looked me straight in the eye and said he just wanted me?*

I glared at his back, as though the power of my stare alone could make the terrifying fae answer my question.

His cloaked head moved slightly, as though he were about to turn back, and suddenly I wasn't so sure I wanted to know.

But he didn't turn to me.

Instead, I turned to Lhoris. "Where are the gold-fae? Why aren't they defending the palace?" I hissed. My voice was louder in the eery silence than I thought it would be, and the female on my right snorted.

She had raven black hair braided in intricate knots, and she too wore a skull mask, but it only covered the top part of her face. "They *are* defending the palace. The gold they keep in the top of their pretty towers," she said.

"Why risk your own life when you have humans to fight for you?" said the other warrior, looking right to grin at me. This one was apparently not fae, from his brown hair. He was a hulking man though, easily as tall as the Prince, and swaddled in thick brown furs. His face paint was navy, a blend of the fae black and human blue, and more intricate than just the usual cheek smears.

"You dishonor our kind," Lhoris spat at him.

He shrugged with a cheery smile. "There is no dishonor here. You make your fate, and I'll make mine."

The male behind us, the warrior with the axe who had come into the workshop, spoke. "Your gold-fae are cowards. Greedy, and stupid. They hole up in their towers, believing that they are protecting what is most important. But they overlooked the rune-marked. Fucking *verslingrs*, all of them." Hatred laced his words.

Was he right? Had the gold-fae really just left the humans to die for them while they protected their gold? They had magic. Humans had swords and spears.

I ground my teeth as hopeless anger coursed through me. I didn't know why I was surprised. I had never been given any reason to believe they would behave otherwise.

We had reached the crossed paths at the end of the palace road. Straight on led to Upper Krossa, where I had been goading Skegin what seemed like days ago, and the path to the right led to the palace stables.

But the left path led straight to the root-river. The one and only way to move between the Courts.

The Prince didn't pause as he took the left path.

It sure as Odin wasn't the way I'd planned it, but I was finally leaving the Gold Court.

CHAPTER 7

I had only tried to get to the root-river once, and sheer curiosity had driven me to it. I had been dying to know what the river looked like. I'd regretted my decision almost immediately.

It was guarded by the densest forest in the whole court, made even more difficult to pass through by a constant thick foggy mist seeping through the heavy trees. I had been rendered first disorientated, and then lost within minutes.

Soon our convoy of kidnappers were forced to pause to light torches, shadow-fae being unable to create like their gold-fae enemies. The female handed the Prince one, giving me a flash of his gruesome mask as he turned to accept it.

Large willow trees loomed over us as we resumed our trek. Hawks and falcons called in the trees, and their prey scurried in the dense undergrowth. The odd wolf howl made it through the foliage and mist to further raise my hackles.

"Reyna, why have they taken us?" Kara's whispered voice was accompanied by an almost painful grip on my arm.

"Your charge is weak, and scared," the female fae said to me before I could answer Kara.

My bubbling rage spiked.

"This path would be unsettling even if we weren't being marched along by four shadow-fae, our fate apparently to be disposed of 'at leisure', as your murderous Prince put it."

She gave a small shrug, then looked at Kara. "How old are you?"

"Eighteen," Kara whispered.

The fae scoffed. "She is no child."

I bared my teeth at her. "And she is no warrior, either. Leave her the fuck alone."

"Silence." The Prince's deep voice rang though the quiet woods, and I switched from glaring at the female to glaring at his back.

We walked for another ten minutes or so, and I gave up on the notion of the gold-fae rescuing us. Gold Court guards patrolled the river, though, and I clung to the hope of them finding us. The mist got thicker the further along the path we got, and I smelled the water before I had any chance of seeing it.

The Prince stopped walking and raised his staff. His dark shadows leaped up and ahead, chasing away enough of the mist that in their wake I could see the dark end of a longboat.

When we got closer, I saw that it was a *karve*. A small war-boat. It was only large enough for about ten, but it was fierce looking.

Where most boats I had seen in pictures had mythical dragons carved at their front, this one had a huge serpent, head reared back and fangs ready. The small sail was black, with the faint outline of a skull on it.

I glanced at Lhoris, his jaw tight.

Where were the guards?

Soft shingle moved beneath my boots in place of the dirt path as we were pushed close to the side of the boat.

"Up you go." There was a shriek and a tug on my arm as the huge human warrior pulled Kara away from me. I reached out, slamming my fist down on his forearm exactly where I knew the sensitive bit of muscle was, to force him let go.

"Ouch!" he said, without flinching at all. He gave me a quizzical look, then wrapped both hands around Kara's tiny waist.

"Put her down!"

He ignored me, turning and lifting her clean over the side of the boat. The female shook her head at me, then vaulted herself over after Kara.

I stepped forward but Lhoris spoke. "Do what they ask, Reyna. Remember our lessons," he said quietly. He cast his eyes to where the Prince was standing next to the carved serpent, his arms folded. Watching.

"Meekness is not one of my strengths," I ground out.

Lhoris held out a hand, offering to help me into the boat. I ignored it, instead vaulting in exactly as I'd just seen the female do. I stumbled a little on the other side but recovered my footing quickly enough that I was fairly sure nobody saw.

"Nice try," the female muttered, pushing past me as Kara rushed to my side. I angled a kick at the back of the fae's leg, but she was out of reach, moving to the snake-head and tugging at the sail ropes as she went. The boat had wooden slats that served as benches across the middle, and large, fitted chests at either end. Oars were fixed at intervals along either side, alternating with vicious metal spikes.

I sat Kara on the middle bench, crouching in the gap in front of her. Lhoris heaved himself into the boat, batting away any help from the human warrior.

"Listen to me, Kara," I whispered. "Just do exactly what you're told. I'm not going to let them hurt you, okay?" She nodded. Her face was pale, but I had expected tears. "You're doing great. Keep being strong."

"Like you," she said, hard resolve in her usually soft voice. Heat rushed my cheeks.

She was trying to be strong like me.

Blessed Odin, I wouldn't let them hurt her.

I sat next to her, but the female called out. "You, up front with me while we push off. Where I can keep an eye on you."

"Me?" I said, though I knew perfectly well who she meant.

"Yes. You. The one who just tried to kick me."

Shit. How had she seen that? She'd had her back to me.

Scowling, I stood up. Lhoris took my place beside Kara, and I climbed over the benches to the front of the boat. I watched as she leaned forward, holding her torch up to a rag at the tip of the carved snakes forked tongue. It caught, casting an amber glow into the white mist. I could just make out the water moving gently before us.

The boat lurched and I stumbled. The female grinned at me. "I'd hold on, if I were you."

I narrowed my eyes at her, then leaned over the edge of the boat. The human warrior had his shoulder against the side of the *karve*, and was trying to heave it forward, toward the water. I assumed the fae male was on the other side, doing the same.

Where was the Prince?

My heart leaped into my throat at a soft thud and a flash of black.

Did he just *jump* into the boat?

Standing beside me, still cloaked in black, the Prince raised his staff. The shadows poured out, whipping around the boat, lending their strength. We moved faster. No oars required.

"Sit," he said.

"No." I didn't have a reason to refuse, other than to prove I was in some sort of control over myself.

"Fine. Fall."

I opened my mouth to reply, but the boat hit the water, and the planks beneath me shifted. I was barely aware of the two warriors leaping onto the back of the boat as I tumbled forward.

A hand shot out and grabbed the back of my shirt, pulling me back before I tipped over the edge.

Adrenaline spiked through me, and I didn't struggle when he tugged me down onto the bench. But as he let go of my shirt, I felt his fingers brush across the rune between my shoulder blades.

Instantly my gold-vision descended.

I turned, startled, and let out a gasp. Drifting out from behind the black skull mask was a single, sparkling, golden rune.

CHAPTER 8

The Prince snatched his hand back, and the gold-vision lifted.

"What—" I started to say, breathless, but his deep voice boomed into my mind.

"Say one word of what just happened aloud, and I will kill the girl and throw her body to the monsters that dwell in the river. Understand?"

I stared into the bright grey eyes behind the mask.

His voice spoke again in my mind. *"Do you understand me?"*

I nodded, still shaken. As I moved my head, unease washed over me, darkness at the edges of my sight.

Oh no. Had whatever just happened triggered the visions?

I braced myself, turning away from the Prince, determined to keep anything I saw from showing on my face, but mercifully, the feeling ebbed away.

52

Silently thanking the fates, I stood up, mind spinning.

I had no magic of my own, only access to the magic within gold, and I only ever saw the floating runes coming from the precious metal.

But the Shadow Court Prince clearly wasn't made of gold. *So what the fuck just happened?*

I gripped the side of the boat, staring out into the mist. I desperately wanted to look back at him, but I didn't dare. Instead, I replayed what had happened in my head. With a bolt of annoyance, I realized that I hadn't got a long enough look at the rune to work out what it meant. In the surprise of the moment, I hadn't stopped to actually take it in.

A regretful hiss escaped my lips, and I saw movement on my left. I stepped back, letting go of the boat as the Prince appeared beside me. He moved like a fucking ghost, and I hated it.

"What is your name."

It wasn't a question.

"What's yours?" I forced myself to meet his eyes, reaching for the boats edge again as we bobbed along the water. We weren't moving fast, but it was enough to make any footing unsteady.

"You may call me the Prince of Snakes."

I pulled a face. "Then you may call me the Queen of..." I cast about for something suitably disrespectful. "Odin's balls."

Something flickered in his eyes. Annoyance, I

assumed. He tilted his masked head backward, toward Lhoris and Kara.

"I can enter their minds and retrieve your name myself."

"Reyna. My name is Reyna Thorvald."

"A strong name," he said quietly.

I frowned. I had chosen my last name myself, since I had no parents, and it honored the ancient god, Thor. It *was* a strong name. But I hadn't expected him to say so. "Why have you taken us?"

"You would have preferred to be slaughtered in your workshop, surrounded by filthy gold?"

I opened my mouth, about to ask why the fuck I had seen a '*filthy gold*' rune coming from him, but his eyes narrowed in warning.

"I doubt what I prefer is of any importance to you. But yes, I'd prefer to have been killed in my own Court than dragged to yours and made to do... whatever it is you plan do to with us." I fought to keep the fear from my voice, the tales of the shadow-fae's taste for torture and mind-twisting racing through my head.

Perhaps Lhoris was right. Perhaps it was time for meekness.

"Not *us*. You."

"Why?"

He stared at me a while, but when he spoke it wasn't with an answer. "Have you ever left the Gold Court?"

"No." I gave him a sarcastic smile. I had no weapons, and no magic. All I had was my mouth, and my courage. I would show him I wasn't scared.

His eyes narrowed. "Who are your parents?"

"No idea. Who are yours?"

His eyes flashed again, this time I was sure with anger. "You are impertinent. All know of my glorious father."

"And your crazy fucking mother."

His staff banged on the bottom of the boat, and I flinched. "She is not my mother. The Queen of the Shadow Court is my stepmother," he hissed.

I raised an eyebrow. So, the mighty Prince of Snakes had nerves to hit. I pressed on. "Same thing."

The end of his staff glowed, and shadows pooled around him. "I am finished speaking with you," he growled.

"What a loss." The shadows tightened, and for a second, I thought I had pushed him too far. But then he whirled, striding down the boat, stepping over the benches like they were nothing. Kara flinched as he passed her, and Lhoris tightened his arm around her shoulders.

"You know, he's killed people for less." The female fae was leaning against the carved snake, looking at me like I was crazy. Or stupid.

"I should be so lucky," I snarled. "What does he want with me?"

She shrugged. "Not my business."

"You just do as he tells you?"

"Each and every thing."

"And you enjoy serving a murderous lunatic?"

She shook her head, a small smile on her lips. "You

believe all shadow-fae are murderous lunatics, don't you?"

"Am I wrong?"

"I guess you'll find out, soon enough." She pushed herself off the snake, and made her way down the boat, after her Prince. I watched as the human warrior moved in the opposite direction, toward me. His weight made the boat tip alarmingly, and I gripped the snake for balance.

"Right!" The human clapped his hands together when he reached the middle of the small vessel. "Listen up, little *gold-givers*. It's almost a day's sail to the Gates. The mists will lift in about an hour. In the interest of making this journey as pleasant as possible," he gave us all an unsettlingly large smile, "I'll do the introductions. I'm Ellisar. That's Svangrior." He pointed at the male fae. "She's Frima." The female gave me a sarcastic wave. "Now your turn." He pointed at Kara.

She gazed up at him. "I'm Kara." Her voice barely reached me.

"Lhoris," said my mentor gruffly.

All eyes on the boat turned to me. Including the Prince's masked ones. "Reyna," I said reluctantly.

Ellisar nodded. "Good. When the mist clears, stay away from the sides of the boat." He dropped onto a bench, pulling something from the pouch on his belt.

"Why?" squeaked Kara.

He looked at her. "Why what?"

"Why stay away from the sides of the boat?"

"There be monsters in the root-river," he grinned.

I turned back to the water, scanning it for signs of life. I could see nothing, but I didn't doubt the massive warrior's words. Nothing in *Yggdrasil* was safe. Danger and death lurked around every corner.

After an hour, the mists did indeed start to lift. I'd spent the entire time restlessly shifting between benches, trying to make sense of my situation.

I'd come to no conclusions, other than I would do my very best to die honorably and make my way to Valhalla. I wasn't a warrior, but folk had been rumored to reach the great afterlife with other noble acts. I would do whatever it took to keep my friends safe and hope the ancient gods smiled down on me.

I heard a loud squawking and looked up. The white mists above us were starting to reveal heavy branches, thick with green leaves. As we moved along the water, I noticed the banks were becoming visible. They were made of wood, winding and organic, and beyond them was glittering darkness.

"It's beautiful," breathed Kara, looking from the thickening canopy of foliage above us, to the darkness on either side.

It was. The leaves of the tree above us glowed with green light, tendrils of mist still creeping across our path periodically. As much as I had longed to leave the Gold Court, I had never really allowed myself to imagine what it would be like.

"Wait until you see the trunk of *Yggdrasil* itself," Ellisar said, looking up from the small piece of wood he was carving with a knife that was too big for the delicate job. He set it down carefully on the bottom of the boat and dug around in a different pouch on his belt for something. Triumphantly, he pulled out a piece of parchment and handed it to Kara. Her eyes widened, then her gaze sharpened.

Kara was the smartest person I knew. Numbers, words, languages — all of it came easily to her. If she could read it, she could make sense of it. She had spent months trying to teach me the ancient tongue, and I ended up feeling positively stupid next to her.

"Reyna, look," she said, not taking her eyes from the parchment. I moved to her bench to see what was on the paper.

It was a drawing of the mighty tree that gave us all life and our world was named for. *Yggdrasil*. Five colossal roots snaked out from its base, rivers running along them, and each ended in one of the five Courts. The Primordial Mists that had birthed the gods themselves were marked above the giant tree-canopy, and within the branches was marked the once revered Vanir — the legendary high-fae who had vanished from existence along with the gods.

"Where did you get this?" I asked.

I'd seen maps of our world before, but they showed the Gold Court as many times the size of the other Courts, and they certainly didn't mark the Mists or the

Vanir. Nor did they depict the gargantuan serpent wrapped around the trunk of *Yggdrasil.*

Ellisar shrugged. "That map's pretty common in the Shadow Court."

"What happens when we get to the end of the river?" Kara asked tentatively, touching the piece of paper where the root from the Gold Court met the trunk of *Yggdrasil.*

"Each Court has a Gate in the trunk you have to get through to get inside. And they are no normal doors, let me tell you. They can't be guarded by fae or humans, because they sap the life from anyone who spends too much time around them. They can be warded with magic, but only so long as the fae have some to spare." Ellisar paused to glance at the Prince. His skull mask and those unsettling grey eyes were facing ahead, and he gave no indication he was listening.

Ellisar continued. "So, the gold-fae pour light into theirs, the fire-fae load theirs up with fire, the earth-fae with soil, and so on and so forth. But they run out all the time." His voice dropped low. "Trouble with the fae is, they get cocky." He waggled his eyebrows, then added in a loud whisper, "and greedy." Kara sucked in a breath and glanced at the three fae in the boat. None looked back at her, and Ellisar laughed.

"Is that how you got through today?" Lhoris said, disapproving anger in his voice.

"Ellisar is done telling you things he should be keeping to himself," Svangrior said, standing for the first time in hours. "I wish to eat."

· · ·

The warrior pulled out a wicker basket from the chest at the front of the boat, and some hard hunks of cheese and bread were handed out.

I considered refusing to eat anything I was given, but on watching Lhoris devour his portion in seconds, I followed suit. It was important to be strong, and I couldn't fight on an empty stomach.

Ellisar grumbled about how small his portion was, his large hands dwarfing the food he'd been given.

Svangrior gave me a sideways glare. "There are more of us for the food to go round than intended," he grunted.

They had meant to take me back with them, that much was clear, but it seemed Lhoris and Kara really were unintended participants in this journey.

Why? Why would they want me specifically? An orphan *gold-giver*, with no notoriety or reputation. My hair made me different, but other than that, I could think of nothing that would made me any more desirable, or valuable, than any other *gold-giver*.

The visions.

The thought crept into my head, tearing a hole in the insistent questions.

The visions of the Starved Ones made me different.

Could they mean something to the Shadow Court? But how could anyone possibly know about them? Nobody but Lhoris knew I suffered them, and even he didn't know the full truth.

There was a small splashing sound, and all the noises in the tree canopy above us stopped abruptly.

"Tell me you didn't just throw food in the river," hissed Svangrior. I turned to see Ellisar looking sheepish.

"The crust of the bread was stale," he said.

"Fucking *verslingr*," the fae warrior snapped, pulling a knife from his belt.

"Don't overreact, we haven't been attacked on the river in moons," the big human said with a shrug.

"You think with your sword, not your head."

"Not always. I think with my stomach sometimes," he grinned. "And when I'm feeling lucky, with my—"

Svangrior clipped him hard across the ear before he finished his sentence. The big man barely flinched, and his grin widened.

"This is no time for games, you fool," Frima said.

I looked at her. She and the Prince had been sitting in silence near the back of the boat for most of the journey. Their matching skull masks looked even eerier in the green light. She stood up slowly, gazing keenly out over the water.

"What's in there?" asked Kara. She was no longer whispering, and she directed her question to Ellisar.

"Snakes."

I glanced at the snake carved on the front of the small *karve*. My memory flashed on the shadow snakes that had slithered under the door just hours before, born of the Prince's staff.

The boat moved ever so slightly to the left.

Ellisar and the Prince got to their feet in a flash, and all three warriors drew weapons.

There was a dull thud against the shallow hull of the boat.

"Fuck," swore Frima.

"This is your fault, Ellisar," snapped Svangrior.

"I was getting bored anyway."

"Bored? Odin's raven, you are like a fucking child sometimes! You—"

The Prince spoke, and the bickering banter quieted immediately. "If anything happens to my charge, the price will be death. Understand?"

My already racing pulse hitched up another notch. *Was he talking about me?*

All three warriors clapped their chests. "Trig!" they called in unison. The ancient word for loyalty.

I shuffled along my bench to move as close to the center of the boat as I could, and closer to my friends. I didn't know what was coming, but the tension in the silence was making my skin crawl and my chest tight.

A thin tendril that could easily have been a long piece of river grass whisked out of the water and over the boat. It hovered a moment, then began to whip back and forth through the air. Probing.

Without a sound, Frima stepped close to it. Silently, she raised her blade, then brought it swooshing down onto the reed.

The response was immediate. And loud.

A screeching noise accompanied the boat rocking as something banged into it. Water splashed up either side of the *karve*, and the warriors crouched to keep their balance. I gripped the side of my bench, trying to keep all sides of our boat in my sight. Lhoris pulled Kara in front of him so that she was in the bottom of the boat, the benches shielding her. Somehow the Prince stayed standing still in all the thrashing.

The screeching cut off, and movement made me look to my right. Something was rising from the water.

CHAPTER 9

If I had to come up with a word for the creature blinking huge gold reptilian eyes at us from the river, "snake" wasn't the one I would have gone for. Fucking *dragon* was a better description.

The thing had a mane of spiky horns around its head, and hundreds more of the reedy tendrils coming from gills at the back of its jaws. It was greenish-blue in color, every third row of scales flashing bright blue.

It opened its mouth, and a long, equally bright blue tongue flicked out. Svangrior yelled, swinging his axe at the forked tongue. The snake moved faster than I thought possible, and more banging under the boat sounded, as we tipped dangerously to the left.

A louder bang brought my attention back to the inside of the boat — to the Prince. It had been his staff hitting the bottom of the *karve*. Shadows swirled around the top, even more than I had seen him conjure so far. He lifted the staff, and they rushed the snake, the force of their movement making his cloak billow out behind him.

The creature seemed to realize too late that the dark, smoky shapes were a threat. It tried to duck down below the surface, but the shadows solidified into hundreds of smaller snakes that wrapped around its throat and then its body, lifting it from the water instead. Within moments the whole monster had been pulled from the river, thrashing in the air and sending water flying. No amount of screeching or movement could shift the grip the shadow snakes had.

"She will suffocate soon enough," said Svangrior, only just audible over the snake's screeches.

The black shadow snakes vanished abruptly, dropping the huge river-snake back into the water with a splash that rocked the boat. I gripped the bench, ready for the attack, but none came.

When I rose cautiously, I saw the electric blue scales disappearing under the surface as the snake raced away. Dark shadows that reminded me of smoke moved around us, filling the sail on our boat. Slowly it began to move, the gentle current taking us again.

I turned back to Lhoris, helping Kara up onto the bench.

"Have you ever seen a fae with magic that strong?" I whispered. The warriors were talking quietly, and the Prince was staring in the direction the snake had gone.

"I haven't even *heard* of a fae with magic that strong," he replied quietly.

Kara was trembling as she squeezed in between us on

the bench. "That thing was huge," she said. "Why did he let it go? I'd have let it suffocate, like Svangrior said."

Her little voice had turned fierce, and I felt a surge of both pride and alarm at her words.

"It didn't need to be killed," I said, then paused. Why *had* the Prince let it live? Surely not compassion. He was legendary for being merciless.

She scowled at me. "What good is it doing alive? It's a monster!"

"It's a predator, and this is where it lives. The lesson here? Don't throw food in the root-river."

"I never want to be on one of these rivers ever again," she shuddered.

I didn't answer her. Given that we were sailing to certain death, or worse, it was highly unlikely any of us ever would be.

The next six or so hours passed with no more sightings of river monsters. The bird calls resumed in the ever-thickening canopy overhead, and the sides of the tree root that held the river rose steadily until we were cocooned in a tunnel made from gnarled wood.

Ellisar's banter had fallen away since the snake incident, and he continued carving his little piece of wood in silence, throwing uneasy glances about. The Prince and Frima had settled at the front of the boat, Svangrior at the back. I stayed in the middle of the *karve*, trying and failing to fight the drowsiness that the gentle movement of the vessel induced. Lhoris and I took turns to doze, whilst Kara curled up in the bottom of the boat.

In *Yggdrasil* you were taught to stay strong. Loss of sleep or appetite led to weakness, and that meant death. But that didn't mean my sleep was easy. Nightmares filled with images of me killing my friends, of having the Starved Ones rip off chunks of my flesh, of the Shadow Court Prince's black mask covering my own face as I drowned in liquid gold, plagued my fitful rest.

A thump on the wood of the boat woke me with a start.

"We are nearly at the Gates." Frima was standing by the carved snake. I looked enviously at her black leathers, the multitude of weapons strapped to her body, and the long braids keeping her hair from her face. She was far better equipped to deal with the threats our journey held than I was. Lhoris and I had been ungraciously relieved of our hammers and scalpels before we left the workshop. My bag remained in my possession though, having been cursorily checked by Svangrior and deemed to be filled with clothes. The staff Lhoris had given me remained unseen, wrapped tightly in my furs.

"Woah." Kara's exclamation made me look from Frima to the view ahead.

I stared at the trunk of *Yggdrasil*. The actual tree of life.

The fact that I was in the presence of ultimate power and magic momentarily cowed all my other thoughts.

Ancient wood rose as high as my eye could see, the surface of the bark dotted with brightly-colored flowers and vivid green creepers.

Directly ahead, set into the bark and growing larger as we neared, were gates just as magnificent as any at the palace of the Gold Court.

They were, of course, made from gold. The two solid doors were covered in etchings showing glorious battle scenes, fae riding eagles and hawks, and raining beams of lethal light down on their enemies. Two ornate golden wings spread from the tall arched tops of the closed doors, nestled into the bark as though they'd always been there. When we got close, I saw two pedestals on either side of the Gates, each topped with a roaring golden lion, their feline faces set in vicious snarls.

Two things struck me as the *karve* slowed. First, the lions looked suspiciously realistic. But second, something was... wrong. Being around gold didn't trigger my gold-vision, only touching it did, but I could always sense it. The enormous doors should have felt like the palace, humming with unspent power. But they didn't. They felt *off*, somehow.

"You feel that?" I murmured to Lhoris.

He nodded, and Kara's brows drew together. "You mean the Gates? They feel weird. Like unstable or something."

Unstable was the right word. I wondered what they would look like through the gold-vision, and what the runes floating from them would say.

If I had some gold to touch, I could find out...

I reached for my bag, but Lhoris gave a loud and unnatural cough. When I looked at him, his expression was severe. Before I could question his reaction, the Prince moved past me, silent and swift. He came to a stop at the head of the boat, lifting his staff as we reached the Gates. Shadows flowed from the tip, easily melting through the tiny gap in the sealed doors.

With a loud, slow creak, the Gates swung open.

"That definitely shouldn't be that easy." The Gates were the only entrance to the Gold Court. No member of another Court should have been able to just swing them open with such little effort.

"Maybe they always open that easily from the inside?" suggested Kara quietly.

"Maybe," I said doubtfully. "But the riverbank should have been guarded, too."

Ellisar spoke. "Your Court's arrogance has cost them." He stood up and the boat wobbled.

"You must have had help from the inside," said Lhoris. Ellisar shrugged.

Darkness moved across the boat as we floated into the shadow of the colossal tree trunk. My eyes moved from the warrior to the golden lions we were almost level with.

"We need no help. You've seen what our Prince can do."

We sailed past the lions, and I felt a tiny stab of relief, which was swiftly replaced by complete awe as we entered the inside of the trunk of *Yggdrasil*.

. . .

69

In the center of the hollowed-out tree was a waterfall, surrounded by a ring of statues of the ancient gods. They faced outward, their backs to the cascade of water. I craned my neck to see where the waterfall was flowing from, but it stretched so high it disappeared into darkness. The light in the space seemed to be coming from the bark itself, a warm, daylight glow that reflected off the smooth, worn stone of the statues. Each effigy of the gods was at least fifteen feet tall, and I marveled at the detail in the faces of the statues I could see clearly as we moved gently away from the golden gates and further into the trunk. Serene Freya with her cats, fierce Thor with his hammer, mighty Odin with his raven.

The falling water should have been loud, it was flowing from such a great height, but all I could hear was a soothing trickle, and there were no ripples or waves in the pool. I peered into the clear water, unable to see the bottom.

"They're so beautiful," breathed Kara. "I don't recognize her." She pointed to a statue of a woman with pointed ears like a fae and beautifully delicate wings. Her expression was serene and wise.

"That's a high-fae priestess." The Prince's rich voice startled me. "The gods called them the Vanir. They were psychic fae."

I looked at him, the pale white of the stone statues reflecting off his grim mask as he stared at the statue of the high-fae female.

His gaze shifted, his eyes meeting mine. There was

something calculating, and incredibly determined, in his look.

This male was not like Lord Orm. Lord Orm was a spoiled, overgrown child, entertained by pushing people to the limits of pain or subservience. This male, this *Prince*, was smart, and I was willing to bet, much harder to please. And I didn't think he would be easy to dupe or cross.

As though he knew exactly what I was thinking, power flared in the gray depths of his irises. It felt almost like a challenge, and to my anger I found myself unable to hold his gaze.

I screwed my face up as I turned away. Seeking out the statue of Freya, almost out of view as we continued our path to the right, I sent a whispered prayer to the goddess. "Make me strong enough to deal with whatever he makes me endure. Give me the courage to do whatever needs to be done."

Even if it was to end my own life, before that of my friends.

CHAPTER 10

The Shadow Court Gates were just as grand as the Gold Court Gates, and significantly darker.

Black, leaden doors loomed high above us, silver etchings catching the light and bringing life to the gruesome scenes they portrayed. Images of battles, and their fatal outcomes, were shown in gory detail, snakes slithering across the battlefields. More images of dungeons, figures screaming, faces twisted, bodies mangled, made me look away.

A snake's head reared up over the gates, similar to that on the front of the boat, except the eyes and the tongue gleamed blood-red.

At a prompt from the Prince's shadows, the doors began to ease open.

The *karve* seemed to speed up, as though it knew it was almost home. We sailed through the imposing Gates as soon as they were open wide enough to admit us, and the air around me changed immediately.

It felt cooler, and sharper somehow, as though something was pricking at my skin. The view beyond the gates was just like that of the root-river on the way in, dense green foliage above us and high brown tree-roots on each side. But there was no question we were in a different world. The bird calls were different, and the damp soil smell that had accompanied us before had been replaced by something sweet and tangy.

I took in a quick breath, feeling my stomach swoosh as the gates began to close behind us.

The Shadow Court.

The realization made me dizzy, as though my brain had refused to fully accept we were truly leaving the Gold Court before. My home, the place I'd lived in, the place I'd *despised,* my whole life.

I'd been keeping my panic at bay, but sailing through those Gates into another world left me no choice but to face reality.

We were in the Shadow Court. Heading to the palace, escorted by the strongest fae I'd ever seen. *And he had come for me.*

Shadows crept into my vision on my right, and when I looked up, I saw streams of dark smoke-like shadow licking over the water.

I opened my mouth to say something, but nothing came out. A strange taste was filling my mouth, something utterly foreign to me. Salty-sweet, I couldn't tell if it was unpleasant or not.

"I—" I tried to say, but more movement caught my eye. The boat was moving much more quickly now, and

I wasn't sure I'd seen what I thought I had. I leaned forward, cursing the dizziness that was plaguing me, and my pulse hitched up a notch as I managed to focus.

A hand was gripping the side of the riverbank. Someone was trying to pull themselves up and over, into the root-river.

But how? How could anything be outside, in the void of darkness?

A head crested the edge, then disappeared from view as we sped around a bend.

Bile rose in my throat.

It had been no normal head. A large chunk had been missing from one side, and a mismatched piece of flesh sewn on in its place.

It had belonged to a Starved One.

How? How could there be a Starved One out here? There were folk who believed they were a myth, it had been so long since one had been seen in the Five Courts.

We lurched around another corner, and big black dots began to flash across my sight. My stomach lurched, the bile burning hot in my throat.

I swore as I stood, stumbling to edge of the boat just before I heaved, losing the bread and cheese we'd been given to eat earlier. I distantly heard Svangrior swearing and saying something about humans and boat-sickness.

I heaved again, and heard Kara's voice, coming closer, trying to soothe me. I felt a small hand rubbing my back, along with more disorientation.

All that was in my head, as my chest strained and my

eyes stung, was the Starved One trying to get into the root-river.

I gripped the edge of the boat, sucking in air, trying to make my words work, and trying to clear my swimming vision.

Should I warn them? The shadow-fae were my enemies. But surely nothing was worse than being eaten alive?

I felt a looming presence beside me and turned unsteadily. The Prince, eyes blazing, stared at me. For a second, in my confusion, I thought I saw concern in his eyes. But then a stabbing pain pierced my skull, and those bright grey eyes filled with swirling shade.

He's trying to get into my head.

The realization was sudden and terrifying.

Fear turned my skin to ice, and I stumbled backward, straight into Kara. Another stab of pain lanced through me, almost making me cry out, and I reached out blindly, trying to steady myself.

"Reyna!" Kara yelped, I felt a physical pain in the back of my skull, and everything turned black.

A dull throbbing in my head was the first thing I was aware of, followed by a strong desire not to open my eyes.

Memories tumbled through my mind, and I gasped in a breath as I remembered where I was. The Shadow Court.

There had been a Starved One.

And the Prince had tried to break into my thoughts.

My eyes flew open, my glare landing not on the Prince, but on Frima.

"She's awake."

"Which one?"

I struggled to sit up, a wave of dizziness forcing me to do it slowly.

"The irritating one."

They were talking quietly, as though they didn't want to be heard, and I blinked around. We were still in the boat, but I didn't think we were on the root-river anymore.

We were moving through a dark cavern, stone walls rising on either side of us, slick with water and covered in inky green creepers.

"What do you mean, which one?" I mumbled, my tongue not working properly and my words coming out slurred and thick.

Frima gave me an annoyed look, then pointed. I dragged myself around on my backside, using the benches to pull my weight. My limbs felt out of place, and a rising panic about my vulnerability was cloying in my throat.

"Kara," I murmured.

She was laid on the bottom of the boat, her head in Lhoris' lap. He gave me a reassuring look. "I am glad you are awake," he said. "Kara is fine."

I frowned and looked for the Prince. He was standing at the front of the boat, by the carved snake, but as soon as my eyes fell on his cloaked back, he turned to me.

Slowly, he moved toward us, the boat rocking slightly.

"You are going to ask what happened, yes?" There was anger in his quiet tone.

I swallowed but my throat was so dry it made me cough.

"I know what happened," I croaked. "You tried to get into my head, and... And my head shut off. So you couldn't."

It was the best I could come up with. And it must have been that, or he had knocked me out by pushing too hard. Could he even do that?

"If you do not know something, why pretend that you do?" he hissed.

Because I hated looking stupid. I said nothing, just glared up at him.

"I want to know what made you sick."

"That's what you tried to get into my head for?" The frisson of fear I felt that he could do that at all made my fingers tighten on the bench. All fae could project images, and it was well known that the shadow-fae could instil fear. But could he actually read minds? I stared up at his fierce mask and burning bright eyes.

I was pretty sure he could do anything he wanted to.

"Why did you knock me out?"

His eyes narrowed behind the mask. "You fell."

"W-what?"

"You tripped and fell, and collided heads with your

friend," Frima said, a smirk on her face. "You have been out cold for over an hour."

I let out a long breath. Guilt over hurting Kara washed through me, but relief that the Prince hadn't got into my head accompanied it.

And given that none of us appeared to have been eaten since I was knocked unconscious, I guessed the Starved One hadn't made it over the bank of the root-river. But that didn't make it any less alarming that one had been trying. I wondered again if I should say something. "Where are we?" I asked instead.

Ellisar lumbered toward me in the boat, handing me a skin of water. I took it gratefully but refused to say thank you.

"My Court. My palace. You will do as you are bid here, or you will die."

"I thought I was going to die anyway," I said after a long swig of cool water. I watched the Prince for a reaction, hoping for any hint of what lay in store for me.

"No, your friends are going to die. I never said a word about your death."

I launched the skin at him. His hand flew out, catching it deftly. Something quirked in his eyes.

"Leave my friends alone," I snarled.

"You understand that you are the reason they are here? If you had just come with me as I'd asked, they would be safe in the filthy hole you call home."

More guilt hammered through me. He was right.

"And this is what *you* call home?" I gestured around the dank cavern. "It's charming."

He hissed, then turned away from me.

"Actually, *this* is what we call home," Ellisar said quietly, and pointed. The boat was emerging from the cavern, and despite myself, my mouth dropped open. Slowly, I got to my feet as we sailed into a world I had only seen in my nightmares.

CHAPTER II

Rising up from the dark water before us was a mountain, topped with a palace that looked like it was made from night itself. Hundreds of tight, sharp spires stabbed at the twilight sky like narrow blades. Sparkling lights, like stars, glittered across the structure, drawing attention to various angular bridges and archways. Below the palace, the mountainside was covered in clusters of buildings, hewn from ledges in the rocky surface. Lights flickered in the small buildings, flashes of color and movement only just visible from our distance.

Lightning sparked in the distant sky, purple and bright as it hit the water beyond the mountain. It reflected off the black surface of the palace, and the star-like lights glimmered every color of the rainbow before they faded.

I had expected the Shadow Court to be gloomy.

Enough light to cause shadow, but dark compared to the brightness of the Gold Court.

It *was* dark, compared to the constant shimmering light I was used to, but there was no way it could be described as gloomy. It glittered just as much as the Gold Court, but in such a different way.

It was beautiful. A word I would never, ever have thought to associate with the shadow-fae or their Court.

I felt eyes on me and dragged my gaze away from the view. The Prince was watching me, grey eyes bright.

I glared back at him, some of my awe slipping away as I remembered why I was there.

His eyes narrowed, then he lifted his staff. Shadows burst from the end of it, moving to fill our sail. With a lurch, the boat sped up. Within minutes we had reached the base of the mountain. The closest villages were on a level carved out of the mountain about six feet above the water, and many long piers led to tied-up boats, some huge longboats, and some tinier than the one we were in.

I expected to move to one of the piers, but the boat angled to the side. The shadows flew at what looked like a jagged piece of rock face, and my lips parted in surprise as they merged together to form a shape that looked like an archway. The Prince held his staff up, glowing, and the shadows rushed back, leaving an actual archway in the rock.

The boat sailed through the opening, and we were engulfed in utter darkness for an alarming moment before the torch at the end of the serpent's tongue flickered to life.

"Where are we going?"

"To the palace. When we reach it, you must be silent. Is that understood?" Frima's quiet words were clipped, and I could see the tension in her stance.

I looked at the other two warriors. Both were alert and straight, hands close to their weapons. I frowned.

Was this any way for a Prince to return to his home, victorious from a raid? Sailing silently through the darkness, rather than parading his victory through the villages on his way up to his mighty palace?

"Are you sneaking into your own palace?"

Frima turned to me with a glare, and in the dim light her mask was enough to startle me. "I asked you if you understood me," she snarled.

"Yes. What happens if I choose to ignore you?"

The Prince answered, without turning. "Then death will be a welcome relief."

I swallowed, instinctively looking to Lhoris. He nodded. "We will do as you bid," he said, and it was clear the statement was as much to me as our captors.

A few moments later we entered a large cavern, long spiky pieces of rock dripping down from the ceiling unnervingly. The boat reached a dark beach at the back, and I wasted no time clambering over the side and onto land. Feeling the sand beneath my boots was a relief after such a long time on the water. And there was nowhere to run on a boat.

The warriors resumed the same formation they had when we had left the Gold Court palace, the Prince in the lead and Svangrior at our back. Frima and Ellisar held torches that lit a steep pathway leading from the cavern, just wide enough for us all. It smelled damp, and the air was cooler than I was used to.

My nerves were tight as we walked, and I refused to give up hope of running. *There's nowhere to go yet, but when we reached the end of the path up out of the rock...*

Except when the path did finally end, it was in an iron-bolted door. More than ten feet tall and covered in bands of heavy metal, there was no way it could be opened by a human.

The Prince moved his staff, and in the darkness I was only just able to make out his shadows swirling into the large lock on the door. There was a loud click, and it swung open.

We emerged into a small antechamber, the ceiling high and walls painted a shimmery gray.

I looked around, trying to spot anything that could be used as a weapon, but the room was empty save for a tall cupboard on one side, made from rich dark wood.

The floor was tiled in white and black squares, and I noticed none of our captors' feet made a sound on the tiles as we crept across the room to the only other door.

We really did appear to be sneaking into the Prince's own palace. *What in the name of Odin was going on?*

Frima opened the door, poked her head out, then

ducked back inside. "Clear," she whispered. With a nod, the Prince pushed the door open. Ellisar handed me something, and I looked down at it. A hooded cloak.

I scowled at him.

"Put it on," he whispered.

"Why?"

"Just fucking do as you're told," Svangrior hissed from behind me. A warning look from Lhoris made my argument die on my lips, and I shrugged the cloak on. Ellisar yanked the hood over my head before I had a chance, then Svangrior gave me a shove in the back. I stumbled and caught up the Prince and Frima as they stepped out into the hallway beyond.

With a significant increase in pace, they headed toward an epic staircase in the center of the tiled hall. I tried to look around, but the hood was so low I struggled to see much more than the legs of the Prince in front of me and the black and white tiles.

"Prince Andask!" The voice was loud and shrill, and everyone halted immediately.

"Fuck," hissed Frima from my right. I looked up, and she elbowed me hard. "Keep your head down," she whispered.

My pulse raced as footsteps approached us. The Prince was obviously trying to hide us, but I couldn't fathom why. Did he want us for a purpose so nefarious that the rest of the Shadow Court wouldn't approve? Was whoever had just blown his secret attempt into the palace a blessing, or would they make our situation worse?

"Is it true you led a raid on the Gold Court?" a pompous male voice asked.

"It is true. Now, I must adjourn to my chambers. I will meet with you later."

"But wait, my Prince, you have brought human captives back?" There was a note of hope in his voice.

"They are for my own pleasure," the Prince barked. Feet moved into my view, bejeweled slippers with steel toes.

"Oh, but Prince Andask, is that what I think it is?"

Kara made a small whimper and I couldn't help lifting my head. Frima let out a hiss of annoyance, but I didn't care.

A small male fae, balding and overweight and dressed in black robes covered in silver and emerald gemstones, was leering at Kara. More specifically, at her wrist.

"You brought us *gold-givers*?" The male's voice was quivering with excitement, and fear caused anger to surge through my gut. He looked at me, and I recognized the cruel glint in his eyes immediately. I'd seen it in a hundred fae, and some humans too.

I bared my teeth at him, and he smiled as he moved his gaze to Lhoris. "Your mother will be pleased."

"My mother is dead." The Prince's words were harsh, and the male moved his eyes back to him.

"Forgive me, Prince Andask, you know the new palace decree. I must refer to our Queen as your mother."

The Prince said nothing for a long moment, and I was sure everyone must have been able to hear my racing heart. "I will present them to her in an hour," he said eventually, his tone as sharp as a blade.

"I'm sorry, my Prince. She is in the throne room now, and I cannot let her wait for this glorious treat." The male's voice was sickly sweet. Whoever he was, the Prince was twice his size, and surely held more authority. Yet instead of smiting him, or telling him to go and fuck himself, he inclined his head the slightest inch.

"Fine. We shall meet the Queen now."

CHAPTER 12

The male's gaze kept falling on me as we followed the Prince away from the grand staircase and toward a set of arched doors at the end of the hall. They were carved with images not dissimilar to those on the Gates inside *Yggdrasil*, and I suppressed a shudder. They flew open as the Prince approached, walking fast and no longer lightly.

The throne room was a mass of darkness, a putrid stench invading my nose immediately. As the Prince's feet met the floor, sconces on the walls flickered to life with flames. They cast shadows on the walls that danced like ghouls across the deep maroon red — the color of dried blood. A shove in my back made me step into the room after the Prince, and my skin felt tight as my breath caught.

A black carpet ran the length of the long hall, ending in a dais and I assumed the thrones, but it was too dark at the end of the room to see.

I could see was what was either side of the carpet though. Urns ran along the edges, filled with human skulls. Some of the skulls were stacked on top of one another, and others were lined up with their mouths facing outward, like silent sentries.

My eyes travelled up at the clinking sound of metal, and my already hesitant footsteps faltered. The ceiling of the throne room was vaulted, but long iron racks hung on chains at regular intervals. And hanging from the racks were people.

They were still, and it was too dark to see if their chests moved with breath. In fact, it was too dark to see if they were male, female, human or fae.

I dragged my eyes away, unable to look. Fingers closed around my arm, and I pulled Kara to my side, making myself look at her instead.

"It'll be okay," I whispered. Silent tears were streaming down her cheeks as she stared up at the racks. "Look at me."

She did, slowly.

"It will be okay. I won't let anything happen to you."

She nodded, and I felt another, gentler press in my back. I threw a glare over my shoulder at Frima, then resumed walking down the soft carpet.

As we moved further in, catching up the Prince, I became aware of the sounds of nails scratching against stone, the clicking of talons, and the hiss and slither of scales.

When we had almost reached the end of the room, two final torches burst to life, each inside the gaping jaw of massive skulls on tall pedestals. Two thrones were revealed, an occupant in the one on the right.

The Queen of the Shadow Court.

She looked like some kind of demonic goddess.

She was wearing black lace and silk, her skirts draped across her knees and her torso elegantly contained in a tight bodice. But scarlet red adorned her clothes, dripping down the fabric. I kept my eyes on her face, refusing to look up and see what could be dripping blood over her where she sat.

She had raven black hair in a hundred intricate braids piled up and knotted elegantly around a crown of ivory bone.

As she looked at me, her crimson eyes widened and her lips curled with pleasure, revealing teeth that were sharp as spear points and as black as night.

"My son," she said as we came to a stop. Her voice was lyrical and soft, but I could feel the magic it carried within it. Dizziness ticked at my mind, and my insides felt cold. Kara made the tiniest whimpering sound beside me.

"I am not your son." The Prince set his staff down on the carpet with a gentle thud.

The Queen moved her intense gaze from me to him. A single drop of red hit her cheek, rolling slowly down her skin. When it reached the corner of her mouth, her tongue darted out, catching it. I felt sick as I watched the pleasure on her face. Kara's whimpering got louder, and the Queen looked at her.

"You have brought me gold-givers." Power rolled from her as she spoke, her eyes not leaving Kara. She looked like a predator imagining all the different ways it could devour its prey. Fear flowed through my veins.

"I have brought myself gold-givers."

"You have creative plans for their demise?" Her voice was hopeful. "I can't see why else you would bring them here, if they are not a gift for your mother."

"You are not my mother."

Something moved in her hand, catching the light. A staff, I realized, but not anything like the staff the Prince carried. It was engulfed in darkness again. "Really, Mazrith, you must get over this. We have discussed it at length, and will again if needed."

I thought I heard a growling sound come from the Prince but when he spoke his voice was clear and calm.

"I have plans for them, yes. I shall see you at dinner." He lifted his staff and began to turn away from her.

"Mazrith." The Queen's voice lost its softness in a beat. I caught a flash of fury in his eyes, before he turned back to her.

"My Queen." The two words were ground out, as though they caused him physical pain.

"Let's kill them now. Together. A bonding activity, if you like." The softness was back, a smile playing on her blood-red lips.

"I have plans for them."

Her smile vanished. "I'm killing them now. Stay, or leave, it's up to you."

"You can't." The Prince stepped forward, and a frown crossed the Queen's face.

"I think you'll find, son, that I can."

There was a silence as they stared at each other, filled only with the rush of blood pounding in my ears and Kara's quiet crying.

This was it.

Whatever was in store for us, it was coming.

Were the Prince's plans for us any better than hanging from a ceiling on hooks, our blood tasted by our twisted tormentor?

Did it matter which of them won the battle of wills over how to end our lives?

Something flashed in the Queen's eyes, and they fell on me. My stomach lurched. A strange restrictive feeling tightened around my throat, and through my icy fear, I felt something even colder on the skin of my neck.

Shadows.

Panic flooded my system, every muscle in my body tensing.

"My son, what you wish to do with your human thralls is your business, of course, but we can't afford to let gold-givers live. Even the pretty females."

"I am keeping her," he growled.

"You want to fuck her?" The Queen gave me an appraising look, her lips curling and showing her black teeth again. "I suppose I can understand that. But still... I forbid it. She dies. She is an asset to our enemy and needs putting down."

The Prince let out a hissing sound that could easily have come from a real serpent. "You leave me no choice." His words were so low I didn't think they were meant for the Queen.

With a rush, his shadows burst up around me, lifting me bodily from the carpet.

An involuntary cry attempted to leave my throat, but it was still tight, and no sound came out. I gasped in a breath, kicking my legs as both Lhoris and Kara cried out. The Prince turned, his black skull mask catching the blood-red light, his bright eyes filled with power. He lifted his staff high and the skull on the top glowed.

"Mazrith, what—" the Queen started, standing from her throne.

"I announce her as bound to me," he boomed. Pain flared in my chest, then a searing feeling matched it on my wrist and shoulder blades.

A cry finally managed to escape my lips, as the pain built and built. I lifted my arm, trying to breathe, my feet desperately groping for the floor a foot below me.

My rune. I blinked in pain and confusion at the mark on my wrist. Black shadows were dancing across the golden rune, almost covering it before the gold burned bright, clearing them away.

The Prince's voice slithered into my skull. *"The pain will stop if you consent to the binding."*

"I will not be bound to you." I hissed the words through my pain and his eyes turned even paler.

"Consent now, and the pain will stop."

"Never."

I had been prepared to run from one cruel fae who wanted to bind me. I would not submit to this one. No matter how much it hurt.

"If you do not consent, I will kill Lhoris and Kara. Or leave them with my stepmother."

My panicked gaze flicked to my sobbing protege and my fierce mentor, both staring up at me with fear-filled faces.

I had already made my decision, back on the boat. I would do whatever needed to be done to protect my family.

With a snarl of pure rage, I submitted to the pain. It vanished in an instant. The shadows flurried around me in one final turn, then they rushed back to the Prince. I fell to the floor, landing on feet too shaky to take my weight and dropping to my knees.

"It is done," the Prince's granite voice sounded above me.

I choked out a strangled sound and lifted my head. Fury danced across the Queen's face as she stared between me and the Prince. Kara crouched beside me, gripping my arm and pressing her face to my skin. A flash of pain seared across the back of my hand, leaving an onyx-black rune etched into my skin.

It was done. I was bound to the Shadow Court Prince.

CHAPTER 13

"What is your game, Mazrith?" The Queen's voice was laced with venom.

"My game is with the *gold-giver*, not with you." The Prince turned to her, then inclined his head slightly. "Mother."

She raised one eyebrow at his word, some of the fury leaking from her eyes. Another drop of blood dripped from above, and I couldn't help lifting my eyes, my resolve drowned in the wake of whatever had just happened.

A man was hanging upside-down from a massive hook, the kind used for fishing whales. A long slit from his neck was the cause of the drip. His lifeless eyes were just visible in the dim light.

I felt my empty stomach roil, and forced my eyes closed.

I would escape this place. Freya, Odin and Thor help me, I would escape this place.

94

"Your father liked playing games, too," the Queen said softly. I opened my eyes and saw the Prince stiffen. "And whilst he often played them with humans, he never played them with the rune-marked. You are playing with fire, son."

"And I will not get burned. She will never leave my sight. But as my betrothed, she will not be touched by a single member of this Court."

Betrothed? They called their concubines their betrothed? Twisted fucks, making a mockery of what was important to real people. Adrenaline was starting to flow through me, now that the pain had ebbed away fully. A sense of recklessness had filled me at his words.

He'd said nobody could touch me.

I staggered to my feet.

"There is more to this than you are telling me, Mazrith. And I do not wish to discuss it with your little friends present. Leave with your copper-haired wench, and let me work out the frustration you have caused me with these other two."

"They stay with me." My voice was louder than I had expected it to be.

The Prince turned to me as the Queen's head tilted to the side. "No. They do not," she said.

I ignored her, instead staring into the eyes behind the Prince's mask. "Go back on your word and leave them with her, and I will end my own life myself." I said the words as quietly as I could, hoping he could read my lips.

Whatever he wanted from me, he wanted it bad, and

95

it seemed he needed me alive. I would do whatever it took.

"Look inside my head if you don't believe me," I murmured. "I've been ready to die since you arrived in my workshop." I'd actually been ready to die since Lord Orm had chosen me, I realized.

"I had an idea last month," the Prince said suddenly, turning to the Queen. "Well, my shadow-spinner had an idea, more accurately. But to test it out, we need gold-givers. If our theory can be proven, then we may be able to create a weapon, using the rune-marked of our enemies."

"A weapon?" The Queen's eyes were alive with interest.

"Yes. A weapon. I hadn't wanted to tell you until I knew it would work. I wanted to present it to you as a gift."

The Queen sat back down slowly. "A gift for me?"

"Indeed, a gift for our whole Court. But I need time to test it. And I need these three."

She stared at him a long moment, raking a black nail down her pale cheek. "Sometimes, Mazrith, I wonder if you truly love me. Today, I choose to place my faith in you. Leave now, and I will see you, and your *betrothed*, for dinner."

The second we were out of the hall I drew in deep breaths, trying to clear the stench of blood and flesh from my nostrils. My brain had gone into a sort of numbness, confusion clouding my thoughts.

The Prince and his warriors moved quickly, and I gave up trying to work anything out as we were hurried toward the staircase. I had to half jog to keep up with them, Kara still crying quietly as Ellisar pushed her along.

My head was spinning too much to keep track of all the corridors and staircases we traveled, and the only thing I was able to take in consistently was the low lighting from the many torches in wall-sconces, casting drifting shadows over the deep-red walls.

Finally, we entered a room that didn't have walls the color of blood. I noticed vaguely that it didn't have the same damp smell as the rest of the palace, either but smelled of wood-smoke and cherries.

The door slammed shut behind us and Frima pushed me toward a padded black upholstered chair. I didn't fight her as she pressed me into it, Kara still clinging to my arm.

"You really are capable of some absolute horse-shit when it's needed," Ellisar was saying cheerfully.

Frima nodded before moving away. "Extremely fine horse-shit," she agreed. "I can't believe the Queen bought it."

I blinked around the room, my thoughts like mud and my stomach sick.

The walls were pale grey, and all the furniture was black, but the large fireplace was lit with a roaring fire, and many candles were burning on the mantelpiece, casting a bright, dancing glow over the room. Thin trails of smoke rose to the vaulted ceiling, dark wooden beams criss-crossing the space. No racks or bodies, I dimly noted. There were lots of chairs, bookcases, and a few embroidered tapestries filling the room, and no bed, so I guessed we were in an antechamber of some sort.

"The Queen is as crazy as a bag of fucking frogs, of course she bought it," said Svangrior.

"I got to be honest though, Maz, I didn't expect you to pull out a binding." Everyone stilled and turned to the Prince, who was standing by the only window, staring out into darkness.

I blinked, trying to keep up with the conversation. Were they suggesting he'd made up what he'd just said about using us to create a weapon?

"Leave me. I need to speak with my betrothed. Alone." He said the word betrothed like it tasted bad in his mouth.

"I will not leave Reyna alone with a monster like you," Lhoris growled.

Ellisar took his elbow, then pulled Kara up to her feet. "Give them half an hour, old man," the human said.

The Prince looked at my mentor. "No harm will come to her. Not if she co-operates."

Lhoris snarled, but before he could argue I spoke. "Lhoris, it's okay. He just went to some pretty extreme lengths to keep me alive. He's not going to kill me now."

"I'm not worried about him killing you," Lhoris spat.

The Prince's eyes sparked behind the mask. "It is her virtue that concerns you?" Kara sucked in a loud breath.

"Leave." There was no room for argument in the Prince's tone. With a roar, Lhoris tried to tug free of Ellisar, but Svangrior took his other arm, and they lifted him from the floor. Frima took Kara, but not roughly. Swearing the entire way, the two males led Lhoris kicking and biting from the room.

The door clicked softly closed behind them, and when I turned back the Prince was standing right in front of me.

"You have questions."

"Yes." It wasn't what I'd expected him to say, but it was true.

"I am curious as to your first."

"What are you planning to do with my friends?"

"Predictable. They will be kept safe as long as they provide me leverage over you. You are extremely transparent."

"Coming from a man in a mask," I snarled.

"I am no man, little *gold-giver*. What is your next question?"

"Who were the men hanging from the ceiling?"

He cocked his head. "Interesting. Enemies of my stepmother."

"Is what you said about using us to create a weapon true?"

"Partly. But not in the way it was delivered to the Queen." *What the fuck did that mean?*

"Why..." I swallowed, almost fearful of asking. "Why me? Why do you need me?"

"You will find that out soon enough."

"Is it... Is it as your stepmother insinuated? You wanted a new concubine?"

He stared at me a beat before he spoke. "Concubine?"

I stared back at him. Did they not use that word here? But the Queen had used it, hadn't she?

"Yes. You know... A mistress. A woman used for..." My face colored. "Pleasure. Because if that's the case, I don't believe you chose well in me. I will make your life as difficult as is physically possible, I will do nothing you ask of me. I will-"

He stepped toward me, holding up a hand and cutting off my growing tirade. "You see that rune?" I glanced down at my hand, where he was pointing.

I drew in a breath, wishing my cheeks weren't burning. "Yes."

Firelight glinted off his mask, and he spoke slowly, as though I was stupid. "It is there because you are now bound to me."

Anger cut through my confusion. "You think I didn't notice?"

"Then why are you speaking of concubines?"

It was my turn to look at him as though he was stupid. "You bound me to you. My life expectancy linked to yours, my will is yours to bend as you wish. My body to do as you like with, along with all your other playthings." My words dripped with hatred.

Something flashed in his eyes, and his shoulders tensed, then dropped. With slow care, he turned away from me and leaned his staff by the fireplace. When he spoke, his voice was quiet. "Is that what they do in the Gold Court?"

"What do you mean?"

"They bind multiple females, as concubines?"

I frowned. "How else can you claim a female and keep her from other males?"

He turned back to me, eyes burning into mine. "You marry them."

Disgust coiled in the pit of my stomach. "You marry multiple females here? That is against the laws in the Gold Court."

"No. A fae may only take one wife."

More anger riled me. "Then you are the same as the Gold Court! Marry one female, bind as many concubines, or mistresses, to whatever the fuck you want to call them, to you for pleasure!" I folded my arms across my chest and glared at him. He would take no pleasure from me, I would do whatever I could to ensure that. Fear that he could force me made my throat close, and I swallowed hard.

He shook his head and let out a long sigh. "No. We may only be bound to one female. I had hoped it would not come to this, but you are now my betrothed."

My head spun. "Wait, when you say betrothed, you don't mean..."

"You will be my wife."

CHAPTER 14

"Your wife?"

"My wife."

My limbs had gone numb, and my brain wouldn't do what I needed it to do. "Your wife?" I said again, completely stuck on the revelation.

The Prince moved to a bookcase, the central shelf covered in glass decanters. He poured something into a tumbler, then came back to stand before me.

"You are the Prince of the Shadow Court," I whispered. "Why in the name of Odin would you marry a *gold-giver*? A human?"

Nothing made sense anymore. Except why the Queen had been so mad.

Fae-bound marriages were unbreakable, everyone knew that. Well except of course... unless one of the couple died.

"You intend to use me for whatever it is you need me for, then kill me."

He said nothing, just stared, an amber liquid in the glass in his hand.

"Why do you have to marry me before killing me? Is it some sort of torture, or twisted mind game?"

"It is my turn to ask a question," he said. "What did you see on the root-river that made you unwell?"

I blinked. That was not the question I had expected. "I don't remember."

"Lies."

"You expect me to trust you?" I found myself on my feet as my voice rose. Fear of him had given way to a panic that was bordering on hysteria. "You have kidnapped me, brought me to a place where humans hang from hooks on the fucking ceiling, I just watched your stepmother licking the blood of a dead man from her face, and I haven't even seen yours!"

"Take this," was all he said, thrusting the drink he'd poured at me.

Without pause, I knocked it from his hand. The glass shattered and the amber liquid disappeared into the thick black carpet.

Without a word, he turned back to the bookcase and poured another one, before returning and holding it out to me. My hands shook as I tightened them into fists by my side.

"No."

"It will not hurt you."

"I don't want it."

"It is the finest mead in our Court. It will fortify you."

"Go to *Hel*."

"I need you alert and able to deal with what is coming, not in this..." he waved his empty hand at me. "Agitated state."

"Agitated?" If I'd had an axe in my hand I would have swung it at his head. "Agitated? You've just told me I have to marry you!" I bellowed. "You're a demented fucking monster!"

To my surprise, I thought I saw him flinch. But when he spoke, his voice betrayed nothing, calm and level. "Drink this and I will tell you what you need to know."

"No. I want to see my friends." I wanted to be alone, truly, but I guessed that wouldn't be an option.

With a grunt, he reached around and picked up his staff. Shadows flowed from the end of it, and within seconds they were surrounding me, forcing me back into the chair. I kicked and shouted, but they were impossibly strong. "You are making this hard for yourself."

"Oh yeah, I'm the problem here," I hissed, thrashing around. After an indeterminable amount of time trying and failing to fight the shadows, I collapsed back into the padding of the chair. The shadows lifted slowly, moving to the Prince. He transferred the glass from his hand to a ribbon of smoky shadow, which immediately made its way to me.

"I will force you to drink it if I have to, but I would rather not."

With a growl, I took the glass. The Prince nodded in satisfaction. "Better. I need your skills to help me with a problem. I do not anticipate it taking long, but I am yet to understand the extent of my undertaking." I opened my mouth to interrupt, but the shadows whipped under my hand, banging the glass against my lips and sloshing some of the mead into my mouth. I tried to spit it out, but the shadows moved my jaw, clamping it shut.

If I hadn't been convinced he was trying to induce some detrimental effect, then I would have savored the liquid; it was absolutely delicious. But as it was, I swore at the Prince as much as I could through forced-shut lips.

"As I was saying," he said. "I will honor my word and keep your friends alive as long as you co-operate with me. You will be treated as my betrothed, given fine quarters in my wing of the palace, and expected to take part in Court functions. I will do what I can to delay our vows until our work is complete."

I tried to speak and was surprised when the shadows moved to let me. "At which point you'll what? Marry me or kill me?"

He stared at me a moment. "So far, you're making the decision quite easy."

I glared at him. "Your kind are known far and wide for your cruelty, and you especially. But I won't let you torture my friends."

His stance changed, anger in his eyes. "You are beginning to try my patience. Your friends are only alive because of me."

"Horse-shit! You barged into my home and kidnapped us and you want me to be grateful you haven't killed anyone yet?"

"I am done talking with you." The shadows rushed back to his staff suddenly, and without another word swept from the room.

Before I could hurl the glass at the door slamming closed behind him, there was a knock on it. Frima pushed it back open, a small human girl behind her.

I struggled out of the chair.

"Come. I'll show you to your rooms."

"Did you know I'm supposed to marry him?" The words tumbled from my lips, and the human girl's eyebrows flew up.

Frima shrugged. "I doubt you'll live long enough."

"Why?"

"Why do I doubt you'll live long enough? You really have to ask? You're a massive pain in the backside. You'll almost certainly get yourself killed, if Maz or one of us doesn't lose our patience with you and do it ourselves."

"No, I meant why did he bind me to him for marriage?"

"Are all *gold-givers* as thick as you?" I glared at her. "The Queen was ready to string you up. As his betrothed, she has no power over you. I thought it was pretty obvious."

"You're missing my point," I said through ground teeth. "What does the Prince want with me?"

"I look forward to finding out myself," she said. "Now, come."

I shifted my stance, ready to argue, and she sighed. "If you come with me, I will leave you locked in your room with food, drink and a bath. Nobody will bother you until dinner time. Except for your new handmaid." She gestured at the girl beside her.

Time alone? That was exactly what I needed. I had to work out a way to escape. And maybe the handmaid could help me.

"Fine."

We walked along more corridors, but no stairs, until we reached a door decorated with a large raven perched on a skull. Frima opened the door. "Don't think about running. Trust me when I tell you, if anyone other than me, Ellisar, or Svangrior finds you, you're in for a world of hurt. And if Maz finds you..." She gave me a look, then gestured into the room. The maid entered, and I bit my tongue as I followed her. "I'll be back to escort you to dinner in three hours."

"I don't want dinner."

"You don't have a choice. The Queen demanded dinner. So, you will eat with royalty tonight."

Before I could say no a second time, Frima closed the door, and I heard the distinct sound of a key turning in the lock.

The maid looked at me nervously. "Would you like me to draw you a bath, my lady?"

"My lady?"

"You should prefer I call you something else?" Her wide eyes blinked up at me, reminding me of Kara. She was not as slight or waspish as my protege, and her fuller hips and bust made me think she was probably older. She wore a clean and simple dress laced over a white cotton shift, and her hair was tied back in a ponytail.

"Call me Reyna. It's my name. What's yours?"

She glanced at the rune on my wrist before answering. "Brynja. Are you... rune-marked?" It was a rhetorical question.

"Yes. I'm a *gold-giver*."

"I'm from the Gold Court too," she whispered.

"How'd you end up here?"

"I was captured. I'm from a town on the outer edge of the Court and the raids are pretty bad down there. But I guess you lived in the palace?"

"Yes. I'm sorry you've been taken from your family."

She gave a tiny shrug. "I didn't have it great, to be honest."

I swallowed before asking her my next question, nervous of the answer. "And here? How have you been treated?"

Fear flicked through her eyes. "I have only served the Prince and his warriors since I've been here, not long at all," she said quietly.

"And..." I prompted, when she said nothing else.

"They have not asked me to do some of the things the gold-fae asked," she said, her cheeks coloring. She was a pretty girl, her round eyes and full cheeks giving her a profoundly innocent air. Just the kind of face the folk of *Yggdrasil* took as an invitation to be corrupted.

I fisted my hands. "I'm glad you have not been violated. Have they beaten you?"

"No more than I was back home, my lady."

"Reyna."

She shook her head mildly. "I'm sorry, but I have to call you my lady. You are betrothed to Prince Mazrith. I would be punished if I were heard to call you anything else."

I let out a long breath. "Okay. Do you know where my friends are?"

"Yes," she nodded. "They are in the thralls's quarters for this wing."

"Are they okay?"

"I believe so."

"Good."

"Would you like that bath, my lady? They have hot running water here." There was marvel in her voice, and I chose not to tell her that the workshop in the Gold Court palace had had hot running water too.

"Thank you, yes."

She scurried off, like she knew where she was going, and I took a moment to scan my surroundings. The room was decorated the same as the one I had just come from, mercifully lacking in red. Black fur rugs covered the floor, and there was a four-poster bed draped with deep purple blankets and furs.

There was a wardrobe and a fireplace on one wall, along with a desk and a bookcase covered in tomes and scrolls on another. The door to the bathing chamber was on the other side, and I could just see Brynja bent over a large claw-foot porcelain tub.

The room wasn't overly large, but it would definitely

be the most comfortable place I'd ever slept. That was assuming I'd ever be able to sleep again.

When I slipped into the hot water in the bathtub, I forced my racing mind to calm.

As methodically as I could, I went over everything that happened since I had stood in front of Lord Orm in the Gold Court. The journey along the river, the gold rune floating from the Prince and the glimpse of the Starved One all seemed like they were a lifetime ago now.

One thing kept pushing through the rest.

Betrothed. Engaged to be wed.

I ducked my head under the water as fury threatened to overwhelm my thoughts again. I took the bar of soap from the side of the tub and began to rub it across my hair, thinking hard.

To my surprise, the more I replayed the conversation, the more I found myself believing that he wouldn't harm us. He, nor any of his warriors, had even raised a hand to us as yet. In fact, I had rarely gone this long in the Gold Court without a beating of some sort.

Not that I trusted him. Just one look at the throne room in his own palace would rid me of any trustworthy notions about the place I was in. I had no doubt he would show his true colors the second he no longer needed me. Whatever I was going to do must require me to be healthy and strong, I reasoned, as I washed the grime from my skin too hard.

Why else would he be going to such lengths to keep me away from his obviously demented stepmother? The discord between the two of them was clear. Perhaps whatever he was trying to do had to do with his feud with her?

But why me? Try as I might, I couldn't think of anything I could do for the Prince that no other *gold-giver* could. That was assuming that what he needed was connected to gold, I realized. It could be something else altogether.

Eventually, I gave up on giving myself a headache trying to answer impossible questions. I needed to work on what was within my control, and that was staying alert, staying strong, and staying alive.

As long as the Prince needed me for whatever the fuck he was planning, then me and my friends would stay alive.

I needed more information if I was going to find a way for us to escape, like the layout of the palace, and routes to where the boats were moored. I thought about how I had planned to flee the Gold Court, relying on bribed guards and stolen resources. If I were to do the same here, I needed to learn about my surroundings, and I needed allies. And I couldn't do that when everyone was watching me like a hawk because I was making trouble.

Lhoris was right. There was a time for doing what I

was told, and this was it. I only had as long as I was useful to the Prince to form a plan and get us out of the Shadow Court.

And out of this betrothal.

CHAPTER 15

When I emerged from the bathing chamber Brynja leaped up from the stool she'd been sitting on.

"Your clothes, my lady." She swept an arm out at three dresses spread across the bed.

My lips parted in surprise as I looked at the garments. "Those..." I looked up at her. "Those are for me?"

She nodded. "You are the Prince's betrothed." She bit her lip, a strange look in her eyes.

"I understand you may need to behave a certain away when we are around the fae, but you can be yourself with me," I told her.

Her shoulders relaxed. "My lady, I have never seen clothes as nice as what's in that wardrobe. My family would eat for years on some of the gowns alone." She gazed adoringly at a lavender-colored gown covered in intricate black lace netting. I leaned closer, and saw that the pattern in the lace was skulls. I moved back.

"Dresses fit for Shadow Court royalty," I muttered. For a moment I considered refusing to wear them. The thought of wearing anything from the Shadow Court, or even fae, made my skin crawl. But when I pictured being dragged down to dinner in thrall workshop-leathers, I realized that didn't further my goal to fit in and keep us safe. It would only draw more attention to how utterly preposterous the whole situation was.

A fae Prince betrothed to a human slave.

I shook my head. "Is there anything without skulls on it?"

"There are some with thorns. And lots with ravens."

There was a tapestry of a raven over the mantelpiece, and I glanced at it. "Did I see a raven on the door to these chambers too?"

Brynja nodded. "I haven't been here long enough to know why, but I think there is something to do with ravens and the Prince's *siv*."

I swallowed at the word *siv*. Ancient language for bride. "I'll add it to my long list of questions about this place."

Brynja helped me into a corseted dress in sage green that went well with my copper hair and amber eyes. It had a low square neckline and the ribbons in the back were pulled tight, forcing my breasts together. The skirt was layered in strips of black lace that did indeed have ravens dotted throughout, but no skulls.

The young maid pulled my now clean hair into a

simple green headband and spent fifteen minutes clucking and tutting as she fiddled with it. She then took two small boxes of powder and brushed some across my cheeks, then dabbed a cold compressed powder on my lower lip.

When I looked in the mirror over the desk when Brynja was finished, I was genuinely shocked at my reflection.

"How in the name of Freya have you managed to do something so pretty with my hair without a single braid?" She had twisted and curled strands around the headband, and my usually pale face was tinged with color in exactly the right places. Combined with the low-cut, fashionable dress, I looked like a member of court. Aside from the unusual color of my hair, of course.

Brynja blushed with pleasure. "I've always been a hand-maid, my lady." Her pleased look vanished as she glanced at the locked door. "Just not here."

"Well, I'm impressed," I said. "Thank you. When I face these fae maniacs, I will not feel so out of my depth."

"You're welcome, my lady."

A knock on the door preceded the sound of the key turning in the lock, and Frima strode into the room.

We blinked at each other. She at my dramatically different appearance, and I at the top half of her face. She was no longer wearing the skull mask.

She was older than I had thought she was, fine lines showing around her eyes. Were they from laughing or scowling? She had scores of braids in her onyx-black hair, tiny skull beads at the bottom of most, and thin lavender cord wound through a few.

"You look different," she said. "Maybe I do know what Maz wants with you after all." Her eyes dropped to my chest as she spoke. I scowled at her. "Come. Maz wants a word before you go to the dining hall."

She led me back to the rooms the Prince had stormed out of earlier, instructing Brynja to stay in 'the raven room' as we left.

The Prince was standing in front of the fireplace when we entered, his staff leaning on the wall next to him. His broad back was covered in black furs and his braided hair fell over his shoulders. Where Frima had purple cord in hers, he had fine silver in his many braids. "Your betrothed, Maz," Frima said with a grin, then turned and left.

"You are feeling better now?" he said, without turning to me.

I groped for my resolve to stay polite and calm. "Not better, no. But less '*agitated*', as you so ridiculously put it."

"Good. You must not refuse food or drink tonight as you did earlier. My stepmother has strict rules, and I do not have the time or patience to repeatedly save your life tonight."

"Are you ready to tell me why I'm still alive at all?"

He half turned to pick up his staff. My breath caught. *He wasn't wearing the mask.*

I couldn't see his face clearly, just a flash of skin in the firelight where the black skull had been before.

"I have already told you." His fingers tightened around the handle of the staff. "I require your assistance."

"With what?"

"I have already told you that I will explain tomorrow."

"Why won't you tell me now?"

He tensed, dropping his head. His clenched jaw caught the light as he spoke through gritted teeth. "Because, irritating human, I do not want my step-mother to dive into your fragile little skull and pull out everything she wants. I need to ward your mind, and I do not feel the desire to do so tonight."

Fear crawled along my spine at the image his words created. But at last, he had given me an answer that made sense. *And a clue.* Whatever it was, it *did* have to do with his feud with the Queen. "Tomorrow, then," I acquiesced.

His head lifted an inch. "So. The copper-haired human named for her strength isn't always deliberately difficult."

I put one hand on my hip. "And the evil Prince who uses shadows and mind games to torture people is able to answer a straight question."

In a flash, he turned, moving just a foot in front of me in a blur of back. My pulse spiked, and when he came into focus, I just about stopped breathing.

Blessed Odin, he was... *beautiful.*

The refined fae prince with tell-tale sharp cheekbones and cruel slanted eyes that I had expected behind the mask was nowhere to be seen.

Instead, I found myself staring at a male who was breathtakingly... different. He was everything I had never known, and somehow so very familiar. His black hair was held back by a silver circlet, and framed a hard, tanned face that had barely a fae feature visible.

He looked like a warrior.

He had no war paint on his cheeks, and his full lips weren't split and dry like the human warrior clans' usually were, but he looked every inch the fierce fighter. My eyes traveled over his face, taking in every thin white scar, a particularly long one down the left of his jaw. His bright grey eyes looked ice blue now the mask had gone, and this close I could see the shadows dancing in them as he mirrored my roving gaze, taking in first my face, then my dress. "Do not presume to know me, little *gold-giver*." His voice was a whisper, and Odin help me, my tongue darted out and whetted my own lips at the sight of his moving. A dark eyebrow quirked, and his bright eyes narrowed.

I stepped back. "Your reputation is famous across the five Courts," I said, trying to break his clearly magic-induced spell.

"I have heard as much. And tell me, do these rumors only cover my killing and torturing? Or do they mention any of my other skills?" The words were a caress, and I swallowed hard. He was wearing a black shirt under his fur cloak, the collar open, and a large medallion around his neck.

I kept my eyes on his face. "Seducing me with magic is akin to taking what does not belong to you," I spluttered.

Something sparked in his eyes. "Do you see any shadows around this staff?"

I glanced at it. "No."

"Then I am using no magic."

I stared, my face heating to the point of discomfort. "You said you needed to ward my mind against the Queen?" I said, reaching for any change of subject.

"Yes. For your sake and mine, do not antagonize her tonight."

Seeing his mouth move when he spoke after only seeing the mask before was having some sort of hypnotic effect on me. The rich baritone of his words matched the face that I hadn't expected.

"Why don't you feel like warding my mind before we see her?" I forced out.

His eyes flicked to his staff before returning to mine. "Just behave yourself. Answer her questions with as few words as possible."

"Is your dining hall decorated in the same way as your throne room?"

His jaw twitched. "It is not my throne room."

I frowned. "You are the prince. There were two thrones in there." Just the thought of the room made goosebumps rise on my skin and I rubbed my arms. He glanced down at the movement, his gaze lingering a second too long on the way back up.

"My father's throne. I will ascend only when my stepmother is dead."

I cocked my head. "Who sits on the other then?"

"Nobody. Not since my father's passing."

It took a lot to kill a fae, especially a strong one, and nobody in the five Courts knew how the King of the Shadow Court had died. Only that his second wife had continued to rule the Court, alongside the deceased King's only son.

"You wish your stepmother dead?" This was exactly the kind of information I needed, and the male behind the mask was proving far easier to probe than the skull-covered monster he had previously been.

"I wish a great many people dead," he answered, and my notions of his monstrousness snapped back into place.

"Rumors say you get your way."

"The rumors are correct in that case."

"Are they all true?"

"As true as the rumors of the Gold Court, I imagine. What did you see on the root-river?"

He threw the question in so smoothly, I almost opened my mouth to respond. "I don't remember. I hit my head."

"I can get the answer myself."

"You already tried that."

"You intend to knock yourself unconscious a second time, to evade my probing? Would it not be easier to answer my question?"

"You answer mine, and I'll answer yours."

"I have answered many of your questions."

"Not the one that matters."

He swept a hand out. "Why you?"

My eyes fixed on his mouth as he said the word you. "Yes."

"You will have your answer tomorrow. And then, you will give me mine."

Was he negotiating with me?

He could just dip into my mind and take the information, as he had proven on the boat. Or, he could stick hooks in me and hang me from the ceiling until I told him what he wanted to know.

The thought made me shiver again.

"That dress is clearly inadequate for the temperature," he said.

My eyebrows lifted in surprise. "I am not cold. I am... unnerved."

"By me?" The predatory look returned to his gaze.

"By bodies hanging from hooks and urns filled with skulls and fae who drink blood."

He stared at me, eyes bright, until there was a knock at the door.

"Enter," he barked. I turned to see Ellisar push the door open.

"You are requested alone for dinner tonight, Maz," the huge human said. I turned back to the Prince as he swore viciously.

Relief surged through me. "I don't have to go?"

"No. You'll eat with-" Ellisar started, but the Prince cut him off.

"She'll eat alone, in the raven room." Shadows were swirling in his eyes, and his measured expression had turned dark. Perhaps the male under the mask could be just as intimidating, I thought as he lifted his staff and power rolled from him.

"Yes, Maz."

"Take her now. Let nobody speak with her."

"Wait, I want to see my friends!"

"This is your fault," he growled. "Do you have any idea how—" he stopped abruptly, stared furiously at me a moment, then whirled around. "Leave. Now."

"Come on," Ellisar said softly, before I could protest.

"Tomorrow," I said, pulling on my resolve to do as I was told. "You'll tell me why you took me tomorrow."

The Prince didn't reply.

CHAPTER 16

T gave Ellisar a sidelong look as we made our way down the corridor. "Why do you call him Maz?" It was probably an inappropriate question, but the cheerful human had so far given the impression that he didn't care much for being appropriate.

Ellisar shrugged. "It's his name."

"But he's royalty. Shouldn't you be calling him Your Highness?"

"He doesn't like being called that. He doesn't even like Mazrith, which is his actual name."

"Why was he so angry about the Queen wishing to eat with him alone tonight?"

This time Ellisar gave me the sideways look, as though this question was stepping closer to a line he wouldn't cross. "The Queen has strong head-magic."

"Head-magic?" I knew what he meant, but I wanted him to be clear.

"She's really good at getting information she wants. But it's not easy. It takes time and no distractions."

"What's that got to do with dinner?"

"The two of them alone all evening means she has all the space she needs to try to pull out what she wants. She was letting him know that tonight would be a war. Maz is going to have to spend all night fighting her."

"Oh."

We walked in silence another moment. "Does it not bother you that there are bodies hanging from the ceiling here?"

He gave me a distasteful look. "What do you think?"

"Then why do you seem happy to be working for him?"

"Because I *am* happy working for him. Now, stop asking me questions. You'll get me in trouble."

"Can I just ask one more?"

"No."

"Please?" I usually only ever used the word *please* with people I cared about. Lhoris had taught me when I was ten that if someone answered your plea when you used the word please, then you owed them gratitude. Which meant it gave them power over you.

Ellisar gave me a warm look. "Fine. One. But I won't promise to answer it."

"Can I see Kara and Lhoris before you take me to the raven room?"

He shook his head. "No. Can't do that." He held a hand up when I started to speak. "They are safe, well fed, and in straw beds." He gave a small snort. "Better looked after than half the Court, in fact."

"Where are they?"

"Thrall's quarters."

"If anyone here sees their runes, they'll kill them for the reward," I said. "They aren't under the Prince's protection like..." I hesitated. "Like I am." *They weren't bound to marry him.*

"Frima's working on that. Until she's come up with something smart, only a couple of folk know they're there." He gave me a sincere look. "They will be safe, as long as you keep your word to the Prince."

"Thank you." The expression of gratitude escaped my lips before I could stop it, but it was genuine. The warrior had something about him that felt real, and I instinctively trusted that he was speaking the truth.

We walked the rest of the way in silence. "Sleep well," he said, before closing the door and locking it.

Ellisar was my best shot at an ally, I decided, staring at the closed door a moment.

I turned back to the room, eyes falling on the bed. Relief at not having to dine with the hideous Queen, or the unmasked Prince, for that matter, was washing the adrenaline from my system, and I was incredibly tired, all of a sudden.

Despite the overly large bed having Odin-only-knew what kind of exotic mattress stuffing and incredibly soft furs, I found myself struggling to sleep. My tumbling thoughts simply wouldn't shut off enough to let blessed unconsciousness take over.

Every creak or squeak from the corridor outside or the gently burning fireplace made my body tense in anticipation. I had gone to bed in a long shift I'd found in the wardrobe, and had my shouldersack with the stolen staff in it under the pillow beside me. I would be ready if anybody came into my room.

Anticipation for whatever it was the Prince might reveal the next morning played against the constant flashes of that unexpected face. *And the reaction he had caused in me.* Whenever I thought about him, my cheeks flushed with anger, and I forced my thoughts elsewhere.

Rolling over for the hundredth time, I let out a frustrated sigh.

It was no good. I couldn't avoid the thoughts I kept shoving away. Not if I wanted to get any kind of rest.

Reluctantly, I lifted my hand and looked at the rune in the dim light. It was solid onyx-black, sucking the light into nothingness. My stomach tightened at the unfamiliarity of it.

I tried to remember the runes that Kara had taught me, and fear trickled through me when I recalled which one it looked like.

Darkness.

The power of the shadow-fae.

Flashes of my visions of the Starved Ones beat through my head, filling me with doubt.

What if there was darkness in me?

I'd always know there was... *something*. Something

that lurked beneath my consciousness, bringing its ugly head above the surface just often enough to remind me I was different. That something was wrong.

And that I had no idea where I had come from.

I didn't know my parents, didn't know why I was the only human in the world who had copper colored hair.

I didn't know why I had the visions.

I'd given up on finding out. I had no leads. No memories of my childhood. Nothing at all to even give me a place to start. Instead, I'd fixed all my hopes and dreams on starting a new life, somewhere of my own choosing. Of escaping the world I had been enslaved to.

I turned over again, burying my hand under the pillow.

Was that why the Prince had sought me out? Because he knew about my darkness? Was I destined to be here in the Shadow Court?

I woke with a jolt, having barely been asleep to begin with. I sat up straight in bed, swiping up a small iron nightlight and lifting it, both for light and as a potential weapon.

But whatever had woken me did not make itself apparent. The room was silent, and I could see movement nowhere.

My heart beat too quickly in my chest, and I wondered if a dream had startled me awake.

Blurry images of men and women on hooks, along

with flashes of the Prince's bright eyes and the Queen's black ones had filled my fitful sleep.

What time was it?

I tried to return to sleep, but I couldn't settle. Every time my eyes felt heavy, images of blood and hooks and dead eyes flashed into my head, forcing my eyes open again.

"You're not a child, Reyna, you can't let nightmares keep you awake," I scolded myself aloud.

The dark visions had given me nightmares most of my teenage years. I couldn't let them weaken me now.

Anger was giving me energy, rather than taking me back to sleep, and eventually I gave up, kicking my legs out of the bed.

It was cold in the room and I moved to the fireplace, loading it up with kindling and coal, before going to the wardrobe and dressing in my workshop clothes. I paced the room, rolling my shoulders and trying to settle the anticipation I felt for whatever was coming when this interminably long night ended.

Something on the floor caught my eye, and I paused my pacing.

Crouching, I picked up the small object that must have been pushed under my door.

A key.

That must have been what had woken me.

Pulse quickening, I stood and carefully pushed the key into the lock in the door. With a quiet click, it turned.

I held my breath, waiting for a guard or someone to burst in. But nothing happened.

I turned the handle and eased the door open. The dark, empty corridor stretched both ways, and I let out my breath.

Who had given me the key?

Did it matter?

I had a chance to escape. And I was taking it.

CHAPTER 17

I turned back to the room only to grab my shouldersack before creeping out into the corridor. Wracking my brain to remember how I got here, I jogged down to my left.

I had to find the thrall's quarters. There was no way I was leaving without Lhoris and Kara.

I roamed the halls, keeping my feet as light as I could and careful not to make any unnecessary sounds. I only saw one guard, a human sitting in front of a large door decorated with a skull. He was nodding his head in sleep, and in the low light provided by the wall sconces, it was easy to slip past him.

I stayed on the level I was on until I was certain the thrall's quarters were not on that floor. I reached a staircase dressed with a plush black carpet. Choosing down, I pressed myself to the wall and rushed down the spiral stairway.

It took me what I guessed was most of an hour, but

eventually, I found a large archway leading into a hallway furnished with a long wooden table. Stations at the table had clearly been set up for embroidery, polishing, knife sharpening, and various other menial tasks. Six doors led off the rooms, and all of them had grates lined with iron bars across the top.

I crept up to the first door and peered in. It was a bunk room, sleeping figures filling four beds. None of them looked like Kara or Lhoris, so I moved on.

I looked through the bars of the fourth door, and the room only held two occupants.

My heart swooped in my chest, hope filling me on seeing them. It looked like Ellisar had been telling the truth. Lhoris and Kara had been kept separate from the other thralls.

The huge, hunched figure of Lhoris completely filled one bunk. Kara's tiny form pressed to the wall on another, taking up barely any space at all. Reaching and scrabbling about for anything to throw, I found nothing. I moved to the table and found a tin of ivory buttons. Picking up a couple, I moved back to their door and threw a button in, aiming for Lhoris.

As I had hoped, the warrior instinct in him reacted instantly. He sat bolt upright, his hands in fists and eyes alert.

I shoved my hand through the bars, waving at him.

"It's me," I hissed, as he jumped up from the bed and came to the door. He gripped my hand through the iron bars, relief filling his eyes.

"You are unhurt?" he whispered.

"Yes. Completely. You? Kara?"

He nodded. "They put us in here, fed us, and have not been back. How did you get out?"

"Somebody pushed a key under my door."

Surprise and then concern crossed his features. "Who?"

"Maybe Ellisar? He has been sympathetic to us so far. And he is human."

Lhoris scowled. "He is a traitor."

"Whoever it was, I don't plan to waste the opportunity. Do you know how we can get you out? Where do they keep the keys?"

He shook his head. "I have no idea."

"You don't suppose..." I pushed my hand into my pocket and pulled out the key that had been given to me. I had little to no belief it would work, but it cost nothing to try. I slipped it into the lock on the door.

Lhoris' eyes widened as it turned with a click. "Odin's beard, somebody in here likes you." He ran over to Kara's bed, touching her shoulder lightly. "Come, girl. We are leaving."

"What? But..." Her sleepy eyes cleared when she rolled over and saw me standing in the doorway. Tears filled them as she leaped up and raced to me, wrapping her arms around my waist in a fierce hug.

I embraced her back, feeling emotion flood my own cheeks, making me hot. "Hey," I said, pressing my face to the top of her head.

"Are we really leaving?"

"Yes. We are."

I knew we needed to head for the grand hall, and the exit. We couldn't leave through the secret cavern we'd been brought in through, since the Prince's shadow magic had created the door in the rock. But, there must be a way in and out. If we followed one of the many stair-cases down, we would eventually find the main hall, and the way to freedom.

I led my friends down the same spiral staircase I'd come down to find them, checking each landing as we reached it.

"I believe the gates to the palace will be on the lowest level," Lhoris whispered.

"I agree. All the way to the bottom?"

He nodded, and we kept heading down. When there were no more steps, we made our way silently along the narrow landing. There were no doors here at all, and the walls were decorated differently, I realized. Still the same shade of dried blood, but there were faint silver imprints on the red, making up images. They were mostly animals. Snakes and ravens I expected now, but there were also wolves and bears and huge lizards.

"I don't recognize this," I hissed at Lhoris.

"There will be an exit somewhere," he murmured.

We made our way all the way down the corridor until it ended in a door. It was made from solid wood, and decorated with one giant claw.

"This doesn't look like an exit," Kara whispered.

"No," I agreed. "It doesn't. But it must lead to one.

Let's go. The palace will be waking up soon, and we need to be long gone."

We pushed the door open, and stepped into the room beyond.

The smell was immediately different. Hay and shit.

We all paused, the gloom thick and hard to see in after the relative light of the corridors. "Stables?" offered Lhoris quietly.

"Maybe." Only, horseshit didn't smell this bad. Whatever made the horrid stench must eat meat, I thought.

As my eyes adjusted, I could make out stalls on either side of us, lining a long path through the gloomy room. Except they looked nothing like horse stalls. They were made of iron bars, and stretched the full height of the room, keeping whatever was inside them trapped.

I swallowed down my building nerves, and stepped further into the room. "Come on. You must be able to get out at the other end."

I looked into the stall on my right as we passed, keeping my fingers crossed for a horse.

It was empty, but the back wall had a large, square doorway, hinged at the top, dim light showing around the four edges. A door for the animal to get outside?

Hopefully, whatever creatures were kept in the stalls were all out there.

We hurried along, all my senses on high alert for any noise or movement that seemed out of place.

Lhoris and I drew up to a halt at the same time, both

shooting an arm out to stop Kara moving any further forward.

"What's wrong?" she whispered fearfully.

"Hear that?"

A snarling, growling sound came from up ahead.

"Yes."

"Let's go slowly."

We resumed moving, but at a fraction of the pace. Every stall I peered into was empty. But the growling grew louder.

Something caught my eye, movement in front of me, and my stomach lurched. I froze. But it was a feather, snowy white, drifting to the dusty ground right at my feet. I looked up and saw a brief blur of white. A soft hoot sounded, and the blur became an owl, swooping in front of us. He perched on the bars of the stall to our left and I stared at him, trying to suppress the uneasy feeling crawling through me.

Owls, in the ancient legends, were guides to the underworld. In this dark and dusky place he stood out as much as I did.

"Perhaps you are a pet of a spoiled fae?" I whispered.

He was beautiful enough to be a prized pet. He had a white face surrounded by a golden mane of feathers, which blended back to white on his lower body. He fluttered his wings out. They were white, too, with golden tips and speckles of gold across the softer down and across his chest.

Dropping down, I picked up the feather that had dropped at my feet. A voice entered my head, instantly.

"Am I mistaken in thinking that your hair is not brown?"

I sucked in a startled breath and dropped the feather.

The owl hooted again, launched from his perch, and picked it up in his beak. Both Lhoris and I had ducked instinctively as soon as the owl had taken off, but Kara was standing, open-mouthed. The owl dropped the feather before her, and she caught it. Her eyes widened instantly. "Erm, yes. Her hair is copper," she said quietly, before holding the feather out to me. "He wants to talk to you."

Hesitantly, I straightened and took the feather from her. "In my capacity as your magnificently wise protector, I should warn you that the gates have been opened," the male voice said in my head.

I tried to process the words as the owl blinked at me, settling back on the bars. "I've lost it," I muttered. "It's all been too much, and my mind has broken."

"Then I will leave now. I have no time for broken minds," the voice said.

"Are you really talking to me?"

His wings folded over his back again, and he shifted his weight between his taloned feet. "Yes. Although the conversation is not promising, so far."

"How? How are you talking to me?" My voice was a croak of confusion.

"As long as you hold my feather, you will hear me."

"Who—, why—" I shook my head, trying to think straight.

"I shall overlook the fact that you are not on your

136

knees, revering me as you should, because you seem fairly stupid. Also, you are about to be eaten."

"Eaten?"

"Yes."

I looked up at the path between the stalls ahead, and realized the growling had been joined by the mechanical sound of metal grinding. Lhoris looked between me and the path.

"Did you just say eaten?" he said.

"Erm, yes. Eaten by what?"

The owl didn't need to answer me. There was a roar, and the most enormous bear I had ever seen barreled out of a stall just twenty feet ahead of us.

CHAPTER 18

I had never seen a bear in real life, only in pictures. I knew they were big, but this thing...

It looked like it could swallow me whole.

The bear was black, but patches of light gray mottled its fur. It stood as tall as my five and half feet at its shoulder, and its eyes were bright, silvery white. It was pawing the ground with huge-clawed paws, snarling at us. Assessing us.

Raising it's huge head, it gave a roar, and my stomach lurched at the sight of its teeth. They would make minced-meat of all of us in seconds.

"Do we run?" I whispered, barely moving my mouth. We were all frozen to the spot, and I got the distinct impression the only reason the bear hadn't charged yet was because we hadn't moved.

"No," Lhoris whispered back, confirming my suspicion. "He will be faster than us."

Kara whimpered. "Then what do we do?"

"You can't get past him," the owl said in my head.

"If we can't run, and we can't move forward, what the fuck do we do?" I hissed.

The bear ducked its head, then reared back on its hind legs. Fear bolted through me, and my limbs almost moved of their own accord. Kara did move, ducking into Lhoris' side.

It was all the bear needed. Its front paws thudded back down to the ground, and it charged.

"Into this stall. The bars are wide enough," the owl called. I turned to him and saw that he was right. The bars he was perched on were wide enough for me and Kara to fit through.

The bear's paws thundered across the ground as I gripped Kara's shoulder and yanked her with me to the bars. I pushed her through with no problem, and before I could even turn, Lhoris was trying to force his huge frame after her. I passed between the bars, then pulled as hard as I could on his arm, trying to get his massive chest into the safety of the stall.

But the bear had almost reached us. Snarling and growling, it raised one paw to strike at Lhoris as it skidded to a stop. Kara cried out as we both pulled harder on Lhoris' arm to no avail.

A blur of white dove at the bear's face, and its swipe was redirected, high above its head. The owl soared out of reach. The bear reared up again, swiping at the bird like a cat playing with a fly.

Using the time the owl had bought us, I darted out of the stall, ran to Lhoris' other side, and charged at him as hard as I could, putting all my weight into the move.

Our combined weight was enough for the bars to finally give way to his bulk, and we toppled into the stall.

The owl swooped in after us and the bear roared as it crashed back down to the ground. The sound of its paw hitting the iron bars made all of us scoot backward, Lhoris and I still on our backsides on the ground.

He was panting hard, and my limbs were vibrating with adrenaline as I scrambled back to my feet. Kara helped pull Lhoris up, and I turned to the back wall, where I'd seen the huge top-hinged doors in the other stalls. This stall was no exception.

My stomach tightened. What lived in this stall? Was it just beyond that door?

It was a way out, though, so we had to risk it. I looked at the owl, now perched on a large metal trough fixed to the bars near the back wall. "What lives in here?"

The owl blinked but didn't respond.

I moved to the door and pushed. It was four times as wide as me and a few feet taller, and it barely budged. Lhoris joined me, and the bear let out another loud growl and swiped at the bars again, making them ring.

Kara joined us, and we heaved our weight against the heavy door. The next time the bear's claws rang against the iron, it sounded different. I threw a glance over my shoulder. He had managed to slice into the metal.

"Push harder," I gasped, turning back to the door, urgency lending strength to my arms. With an almighty effort, we managed to get the bottom of the door to move a few feet. Hope filled me, but then something hit the other side, forcing us all stumbling backward, toward the bars and the bear.

"What was that?" squealed Kara, as the door swung on its top hinge. Whatever was on the other side made a loud hissing sound, and the bear roared in response.

"Push back!"

We all scrambled back to the door, throwing our weight against it, no longer trying to open it but to stop whatever was on the other side from getting in.

I looked over at the owl. "Any more bright ideas?"

He hooted, and looked pointedly at where the bear's feet were churning up the dust outside the bars. The white feather was lying on the ground.

"I'm not going to get it," I breathed.

The bear swiped again at the bars, claws lodging in the failing metal. One of the iron rods gave up its fight and clattered to the ground.

"Odin help us," Lhoris said through gritted teeth.

But Odin hadn't been seen in centuries. We were trapped, and no ancient god was about to stop us becoming bear food.

A male voice rang through the air. "Arthur!" Pounding footsteps accompanied the shout, and the bear rocked back onto its haunches, turning his huge head.

Svangrior skidded into view on the other side of the bars, shadows whirling from his staff. The bear let out a reluctant wail, then fell back onto all fours.

"What in the name of Thor do you think you're

doing!" The fae bellowed at us. He held up his staff, and the bear backed up, ducking his head.

I never thought I'd be grateful to see a shadow-fae.

"Get the fuck out of that stall, now!" Some of the shadows zoomed into the stall and filled the gap around the door, sealing it.

None of us hesitated to do as we were told. It took a moment to get Lhoris back through the bars, by which time Svangrior had backed the bear another ten feet down the path.

My heart was hammering against my ribs, and my breath was coming short.

We were all alive, and in one piece — an outcome I had seriously doubted just moments ago. *But we had been caught.* And not just by anyone, but by one of the Prince's own warriors.

Our attempt at freedom had been thwarted. Anger and disappointment coursed through me, along with a healthy dose of anxiety. Svangrior wouldn't kill us, he knew we were too valuable to his master. But what would the Prince do when he found out?

"I'm sorry," I whispered to the others. Svangrior maneuvered the bear into a stall, muttering soothingly to it the whole time.

Kara looked up at me with a resolute expression on her wide-eyed face. "We didn't get eaten," she whispered. "So it was worth a try."

I swallowed. She might not think so after the lashing that was sure to come our way. I would do what I could to take the brunt of the punishment.

Lhoris squeezed my shoulder and I looked at him. "I got it wrong, Lhoris. I'm sorry, for whatever comes next."

"Die trying," he said. A motto of his clan. And his way of saying it wasn't my fault.

I nodded. "We'll get out."

Svangrior strode back toward us, fury burning in his gaze. "Out. Now." He directed his staff at the door we'd entered through, and we all turned obediently.

The fae didn't say a word as he marched us back to the thrall's quarters. The longer we walked, the more nervous I became.

He locked Lhoris and Kara back in their room without breaking his silence, then marched me on mutely. When we reached the corridor I recognized as the one that housed my room, I spoke.

"It was all me," I said. "They did nothing. Only I need be punished."

"How did you get out of your room?"

"I can pick locks," I lied.

"Do you understand what would have happened if you had died? Do you understand what Maz would have done?"

A swirl of defiance broke through my nerves. "No, I do not fucking understand. Because I have no idea why I've been brought here. It's not my problem if your master can't use me for whatever twisted game he's playing."

143

Svangrior swung to face me, and I stopped walking abruptly. "He has been looking for you—" he hissed, then broke off, shaking his head. "If that bear had pulled you apart, then Odin help me, the whole Court would have felt his wrath."

I screwed my face up in anger. "Are you seriously telling me that I have a duty to stay alive, *for him and your Court*?"

"Stay in your accursed room," he spat. "It will be locked with magic from now on. I will not tell Maz about this, because I don't want to deal with his fucking temper."

My argument died on my lips. He wasn't going to tell the Prince? "Does that mean my friends won't be punished?"

"Unless you try to escape again. And if you do,"—his eyes blazed with anger,—"then their fate will be far worse than Arthur ripping them limb from limb, let me tell you. I will ensure you suffer nightmares about your part in their death for the rest of your sorry life."

CHAPTER 19

I collapsed onto my bed, wishing my pulse would slow.

Here I was, locked in my room again, my escape attempt an utter failure. I sat up, rubbing my hands across my face and trying to pull anything useful out of the last few hours.

I had seen Lhoris and Kara, and they were safe. That was the most important thing.

Also, I had a friend here. Someone had pushed the key under my door. My room would be locked with magic from now on, so getting out was no longer an option, but still, someone in the palace had tried to help me.

And there was the owl.

He had said something about being my protector, and mentioned the color of my hair. How was that even possible?

Adrenaline was still flowing through my body,

making me twitchy and unable to focus. In a few hours, the Prince was coming for me, and I would find out what I had been kidnapped for. I needed to be alert and ready, not strung out and exhausted.

"Get it together Reyna. One thing at a time," I told myself aloud, before going into the bathing chamber and washing my face with warm water, trying to relax my racing thoughts.

I was no worse off than I'd been before. Just a little shaken up. I would be ready to face the Prince — who would know nothing of what had just happened.

I took deep breaths as I looked at myself in the mirror over the basin.

My reflection showed a woman in the wrong place.

It always had, but the obviousness of my not fitting in was even more pronounced here, in this dark and cold palace. I picked up a strand of shining copper hair, the low firelight in the chamber making it glow in the gloom.

"You can do this, Reyna. Do as you're told. Find your allies." But before I could add, 'escape' to the end of my sentence, Svangrior's words floated back.

If I tried to escape again and was caught...,

I closed my eyes.

I wouldn't give up.

Die trying.

But next time, I would make sure we weren't caught.

When I walked back into the bedroom, I froze.

There was a large white and gold owl perched on the corner post of my bed.

"H-hello," I said slowly. "How did you get in here?"

The owl blinked at me. Without warning he flew from the post, toward the fireplace. With a small, angry hoot, he dove at the tapestry that depicted the black raven, then flew back to the post.

"You don't like ravens? I think you're in the wrong room then." Again, he flew to the tapestry and pecked hard at the raven. This time, he caught a bit of the material in his beak, and when it came away from the wall, I saw the tiniest flash of something.

I stepped to the tapestry and cautiously lifted it from the wall. The owl flew back to the post, watching me.

A window. There was a window behind the picture.

I examined the heavy artwork, trying to see how it could be removed from the wall, and then I saw a sturdy, but fine, piece of cord hanging from the rod it was fixed to at the top. I pulled on it, and the tapestry began to roll up from the bottom on some sort of pulley.

I kept pulling until the whole thing was in a neat roll at the top of a small, arched window. The panes of glass were criss-crossed with lead piping, and the window was set high enough into the wall that I had to stand on tiptoes to look out. There were courtyards far below, not filled with white marble and gold like the ones at home but with large stone statues of dragons and serpents, and the odd raven. Beyond that, much lower, I could see the twinkling lights of towns. The sky was the same dusky twilight it had been when we arrived, sprinkled with pinpricks of light.

Dragging my eyes from the view, I looked for a catch on the window. There was no way I could escape out of it, the drop to the courtyard below was completely sheer. But it must have been how the owl had gotten in.

Try as might though, I couldn't find a catch. All that was on the sill was one snowy white feather with a dusting of gold.

I picked up the feather and turned to the owl. "Thanks for the help with the bear," I said. It wasn't actually what I'd intended to say, but without the owl's distraction, Lhoris would definitely not have made it through the night in one piece.

The owl blinked. "I am a mighty warrior. It was not difficult."

Despite everything, the corner of my mouth lifted in a smile. The bear had been at least twenty times the size of the owl. "Well, all the same. I appreciate it. How did you get in here? The window doesn't open, and the door is locked."

"I was hunting in the forest when I was visited by a fae. She told me I was to assist the copper-haired gold-giver in whatever way was needed. Then I found myself here. I assume you to be the copper-haired gold-giver?"

I nodded slowly, nerves tingling through me. "Who was the fae?"

"I do not know. She was..." The owl tilted his head thoughtfully. "Magical and moderately terrifying. Almost as terrifying as I am when I hunt."

"Terrifying?"

"Yes. Also, my hunt was not finished, and I am hungry. Where do you store your rodents?"

I shook my head again, then sat down on the chair. "Why were you told to assist me?"

"I do not know. I assume you require my superlative hunting skills?"

"I.... Well...no. I don't think so."

He hooted irritably. "Then why was I sent here? To save you from marauding bears?"

"I honestly have no idea. What did the fae say to you?"

"I already told you that." He blinked his perfectly round eyes. "My initial suspicion that your intellect is far below mine is proving to be correct. Disappointing."

I drew in a long breath. "What's your name?"

"Voror."

"Okay. I'm Reyna."

"I shall call you *heimskr*."

"I am not stupid," I told Voror, taking another deep breath.

"You have an understanding of the ancient language? That does not fit with the idiocy you have so far presented."

"Can you just call me by my name?"

"No."

I folded my arms. "How is it *you* can speak the ancient language?"

"I am of superior intellect."

"You're an owl."

"A superiorly intellectual owl."

"Could you speak before this mysterious fae visited you?" I asked him.

"Of course I could."

"To humans?"

The owl paused before answering. "No. To a select few fae."

"Which fae?"

"The royal family of the Earth Court."

"Is that where you live?"

"No."

"Then why do you speak to them?"

"I don't."

My jaw clenched tight. "You just said you did."

"No. I said I could have, if I wanted to. They are the only magic users in the five Courts equipped to converse with creatures as intelligent as myself."

I ground my teeth. "Do you not find it strange that you can talk with me then?"

"No. The fae told me to give you the feather."

"So you haven't told me everything she said!" I exclaimed, standing up.

He ruffled his wings, shifting his weight again. "If you find me a rodent, I will recount the conversation word-for-word."

I pinched my nose. "I don't have any rodents in here."

He hooted haughtily. "Then I shall bid you good-night." He spread his wings wide and took off from the post.

I cried out as he headed straight for the closed

window, but the sound died on my lips when he passed straight through the glass.

"What the..." I stood up as high on my tiptoes as I could to look out of the window and watched him swoop away, down toward the closest town.

I paced the room for the next half an hour, trying not to freak out that a second unknown fae was aware of the 'copper-haired gold-giver'. The Prince had sought me out. And now this owl had been sent to find me by somebody different. What did they know about me that I didn't?

A heavy truth was trying to settle over me, invading my brain, and my stubborn defiance was failing in its attempt to dislodge its hold.

It was no good.

I stopped pacing, and let the words whisper into my head.

I can't run from this.

Both because of Svangrior's threat to my friends, and because I needed more information.

I needed to know why the Prince had sought me out. I needed to know who the fae who had sent Voror was, and what they knew. And I needed to find out what my part in whatever this was, before I could make any kind of bid for freedom.

Movement made me look at the window. Voror drifted through the glass, then landed gracefully at the end of the bed.

I picked up his feather from where I'd put it on the desk. "You're back."

"I have completed my hunt," the owl announced, ruffling his feathers. "And now, as promised, I shall tell you what the fae female said to me, word-for-word. She said: Voror, mighty and wise owl. You are required by the ancient ones to assist the copper-haired gold-giver. Give her one of your feathers and she will be able to communicate with you. This is a dangerous quest that could change the course of *Yggdrasil's* future, and the fate of all the fae and humans who call it home. Good luck."

My eyebrows shot up as I gaped at him. "Ancient ones? Change the course of *Yggdrasil's* future?"

"That is what she said."

"What kind of fae was she?" Desperation to know more was burning through me.

"I do not know."

"Well, what color hair did she have?" That was usually a sure way to tell what kind of magic a fae had. Ice-fae had blue hair, gold-fae had white, and so on.

"Her hair was... made of light."

"What?"

"Do you have problems with your hearing, or is it your inferior intellect that requires me to repeat myself so often?" I narrowed my eyes at the owl, and he shrugged his feathers. "It was made of light. My sensitive, superior, eyesight struggled. A little."

"Do you know of any fae who have hair made of light?"

"No. Or I would have answered your earlier question about what kind of fae she was." His tone was dry.

"Voror, I've had a long day. A long *few* days. I've been kidnapped. I'm supposed to marry a murderous maniac —at least until I help him with some secret plot, after which he'll probably kill me. And now you're telling me I'm connected to the fate of the whole of *Yggdrasil*. Oh, and I almost got eaten by a bear a couple of hours ago. I'm going to need a little longer than usual to process information. Okay?"

The owl tilted his head. "Humans are strange."

"No doubt." I rubbed my hand over my face yet again. "How did you fly through the window when it was closed?"

"The fae female made me glow. And now I can fly through solid objects."

I blinked at him. "That could be useful." It meant he could go anywhere in the palace. Except that the shadow-fae might notice a big white owl flying around.

"It does not help me catch rodents."

"Perhaps not. But it might help you in your quest to assist the copper-haired gold-giver."

"I do not know why I have been selected for such a task. I was perfectly happy in my forest."

I had no idea why either. But I did know I needed allies. And someone, somewhere, had sent him to help me.

Could they be trusted?

The memory of Voror diving at the colossal bear, saving Lhoris' life, filled my head.

Making a quick decision, I launched a flattery offensive, knowing it would be the easiest way to get on the right side of the self-important bird.

"I'm sure your forest is missing you. Except all the rodents. They must be celebrating the absence of such a formidable hunter."

Voror's feathers ruffled proudly. "I imagine that they are, yes."

"And I'm sure the fae selected you for a good reason. She must have known you were the only one who could be trusted with the fate of *Yggdrasil*."

He blinked at me. "Well, of course she did."

"Listen, the Prince is going to tell me why I'm here in a few hours. But I don't think we should let him see you."

"I am hard to miss, in all my glory."

"Are you adept at hiding?"

"An owl cannot hunt, if they cannot be stealthy," he said drily.

"Good, then hide. Come back later."

"Fine. In the meantime, find a way to keep my feather on your person, so that I may contact you at will."

"Good idea."

"I am an endless well of good ideas."

"I'm sure you are."

Without another word, he flew out of the closed window.

CHAPTER 20

I was relieved when there a knock on the door a short while later, followed by Brynja's voice. "Morning, my lady."

The door to my room swung open and the maid stepped through, before it slammed closed again.

"Brynja," I said. "Who just opened that door?"

"Frima, my Lady." She was carrying a tray laden with bread and fruit, which she set down on the desk. "The Prince is coming for you in half an hour, so we must dress you," she said, kind of apologetically.

"I am dressed," I said, trying to dispel the ominous feeling that came with her words.

She shook her head. "In a dress, my Lady. As is fitting for a female of Court."

I sighed. I needed to know what I was here for. And I needed no more enemies. If I had to wear a dress to prove I was toeing the line, I would do so.

I ate as much of the food that Brynja had bought as I

155

could in the limited time I had, while she prepared a dress that was simpler than the one from the previous night, in a pale lavender. It had a higher neckline, but it was lightweight, and I was pleased with how easily it moved once I had it on. If I needed to run, I would be able to. She was standing behind my chair, doing something time-consuming with my hair, when I remembered Voror's feather.

"Brynja, I have a white feather over there. Do you think you could fashion it into my hair?"

"Oh. If you really want me to," she said doubtfully.

"I'd be grateful."

"Of course, my lady."

When she was done, and I looked in the mirror I saw that she had managed something clever with a plain black headband, and tucked the feather in so that most of it was hidden between my thick copper hair and my ear. The top of the feather poked out artfully though, as though it was supposed to be there for decoration.

"It looks great. You're really good at this."

The maid blushed and gave me a small curtsey. "Thank you, my lady."

I let out a sigh. "I'm not going to get used to you calling me that."

"I'm sorry, my lady."

A sharp rap on the door cut us both off. Butterflies flitted through my stomach.

Before the maid could reach the door, it banged open.

The Prince of the Shadow Court stepped into the room, staff in hand. He was dressed the same as he had been the day before, and I realized I had almost been hoping he would be wearing the mask.

His bright gaze fell on me immediately, the intense look matched by the scarred but so very beautiful face.

"Leave," he barked, flicking his eyes to Brynja.

I scowled as the maid squeaked, then fled the room.

Say nothing, I chanted in my head. My goal was to get information and allies. Not to be difficult. All fae treat humans like shit. I couldn't stop him being a dick to the maid.

"Sit."

"Good morning," I said, instead of sitting.

His eyes narrowed. "It is a piss-poor morning."

"You're not the one who's been kidnapped and forced into marriage and/or death."

Well, at least I'd managed two polite words.

"Sit," he barked, louder.

"Why?" *Reyna! Just do as you're told!* I chided myself mentally, even as I stared defiantly at him.

"I need to ward your mind against my stepmother."

My chin ducked defensively. "Does that mean you have to get into my head?"

"Yes."

"Then, no."

He bared his teeth at me, and the few refined fae features that did show on his face vanished. He was every inch the warrior. "I am not playing games with you this morning. Sit the fuck down."

Shadows swirled from his staff, and I knew what was coming next.

Power emanated from him, angry and taut, and enough to cause tendrils of fear to creep through my body.

Any patience or tolerance I had seen up to now had gone from him completely, and I knew I would not be safe pushing him today.

Did he know about my failed escape attempt?

Ellisar's words came back to me.

He will be in a fight with the Queen all night.

I took a breath as the shadows moved toward me, ready to pin me to the chair.

"I don't want to fight with you."

He paused. "Why do I not believe you?"

"I just don't want you in my head. Is there any other way?"

He stared at me, the shadows hovering between us. "Tell me what you saw on the riverbank," he said eventually. His tone was hard.

"Why do you want to know so much?"

"If you do not want to fight with me, prove it. Tell me what I want to know."

"I don't remember."

The shadows rushed me. "You have chosen the wrong fae to fight with on the wrong day," he snapped, as I cried out.

"I chose none of this!"

"You think I did?"

I stopped struggling long enough to glare at him. "If you didn't choose this, why the fuck are you doing it?"

He bared his teeth again, snarling. "If you choose to

fight with me you will lose. And trust me, it will hurt. Stop lying to me."

Resolve whirred through me, accompanied by a healthy dose of fear. *Don't be difficult. Get information and allies. Don't get tortured by the Prince of the Shadow Court.*

"I'll tell you, if you agree to stay out of my head."

If he got in my head, he could see so much more than the riverbank. He could see everything. He could see my attempt to escape the night before. *He could see what I saw in my visions.*

"If you lie to me..." he let the sentence trail off, his shadow snakes still pinning me to the chair and shade dancing across his bright eyes.

"Do we have a deal?"

He nodded tightly. "What did you see?"

"A Starved One."

The snakes slackened instantly, then rushed back to his staff. I kept my eyes on his face, but other than a tightening of his jaw, saw no reaction.

"Describe what you saw, exactly," he said.

"I saw a hand, then a head come over the edge."

"How do you know it was a Starved One?"

I pulled a face. "Because its head was sewn together."

Some of the tension in his jaw lessened, and he muttered something I couldn't quite catch. Something about elders.

"Are Starved Ones common in the Shadow Court?"

"No."

"How was it out there in the void? Is that where they live?"

"I don't know how it was in the void."

"But you know where they live?"

His eyes narrowed. "Enough talk of those vile creatures." He held his hand out. "Give me your headband."

I moved my hand to my head. "My headband? But, I don't know how to put it back on. The maid did it," I said, feeling a little stupid. Also, I didn't want him to think there was anything strange about the feather tucked into it.

"Then come here."

I stood slowly, nerves skittering through me. "You swear you're not going to get in my head?"

"My word means nothing to you."

"That doesn't stop you offering it."

"Unlike the filthy fae of your Court, it does stop me. I will not give sacred words to one who holds me in such low regard."

I blinked. Again, he was suggesting it was my fault that I didn't trust him. "You do realize that you have told me repeatedly that you're going to kill me and my friends?"

He glared back at me. "And you do realize that I made you my betrothed to save your cursed life?"

I stared at him in disbelief. He genuinely expected my gratitude. The male was delusional. But in his own fucked up way, I was starting to believe that he was at least honest.

"Ward my headband, or whatever it is you need to do," I said. There was no point arguing with him, and I wanted it over and done with.

With a small snarl, he stepped close to me. He was so much taller than me that my eyes were level with his massive chest. The smell of woodsmoke and cherries washed over me, and as he raised his hand to the side of my head, I had the most insane urge to step into his solid body.

You should be running away, not toward him!

Heat flushed my face and I snapped my eyes closed to stop them moving to his face.

It must be part of his magic, I told myself, as I felt his fingers touch the band on my head. A cool breeze swirled around me, and I knew it was his shadows. Heat flared suddenly across my skull, and my eyes flew open instinctively.

Gold runes.

Two of them, burning bright on his collar bone, before drifting off his skin and floating away into nothingness.

I looked up at him, open-mouthed, and this time I did take a step back. There was hunger in his face. An intense desire that was unquestionably aimed at me.

It vanished as his hand snapped back from my hair, and his expression turned hard. But it was too late. The look was seared into my mind, and Odin help me, I already wanted to see it again.

"How are you doing this?" I whispered, taking another step back.

"I am warding your mind against my stepmother. Wear that headband, always, and she will struggle to get into your thoughts." His words were stilted, and I shook my head.

"No, not that. How are you doing..." I lifted an unsteady hand, my face so hot it was uncomfortable. "The other thing."

"I don't know what you're talking about."

He was lying. He had to be.

"Why are there gold runes on you?"

He was back in front of me in a flash, his shadows billowing out and surrounding me completely. Faint screams began to echo in the distance, and my skin felt like I had been doused in ice.

"Never, ever mention that inside these walls," he boomed, and the voice was inside my head. I blinked terrified eyes up at his own, which were swirling not with smoke-like shade, but actually filled with writhing black snakes.

I nodded, desperate for him to back off, for the fear to stop.

He did, and the warmth of the room seeped back over me as I sucked in a shaky breath.

"We leave now," he barked, and whirled away, striding from the room. Warm air filled the space he had left, the suffocating fear flowing away. Relief that I could no longer see his face washed through my pounding body.

If I had needed a reminder that he was a monster, I had just been given it.

CHAPTER 21

When I felt steady enough, I followed the Prince out of the room. He was waiting in the corridor, his shadows gone but his stance tense.

"Where are your warriors?" My voice was smaller than I wanted it to be, and I tried to steel my nerves. "And why are all the walls here the color of blood?"

He turned and started to walk. I moved quickly to keep up with his long strides, trying to pay careful attention to the turns we took.

"My stepmother decorated."

"And your warriors?"

"Enough talking."

My pulse quickened as we headed down a spiral staircase that was distinctly familiar.

Was he taking me back to the monster-filled stables to punish me for last night?

Relief coursed through me when he stepped off the staircase before the bottom level, heading down a wide corridor. We walked past a few old and battered looking doors, until he stopped in front of one. The iron hinges looked bent and broken, the wood was scratched, and there was no door handle.

He held his staff up, and shadows snaked out form it, flowing into the gap around the door. They glowed silver briefly, and then the door swung open.

When I stepped through after him, I saw a dark cavern carved out of the rock of the mountain, like the one we had come to the palace through. There was a tiny boat on the little beach, and the Prince stepped into it. I followed him, and his shadows flowed to the little sail, swelling it enough that we moved easily onto the inky water.

We sailed across the pool that filled the cavern, until we reached a crevice in the rock. A narrow river flowed gently into the mountain itself. Claustrophobia pressed in on me as we sailed into it, the space barely wide enough for the boat.

"Where are we going?" My quiet words echoed off the stone walls.

When the Prince turned to me, his eyes were brighter than our surroundings, as though they had their own light. "Nobody knows of this place. You must never speak of it."

"Is that why you warded my mind against the Queen? You don't want her knowing about it?"

"Yes."

"What about your warriors?"

"They cannot know either. Nobody must know."

I raised my eyebrows. Surely he was giving me something I could leverage? Why would he risk telling his secrets to me? "Why am I here?"

"You will see soon enough."

We traveled on in silence, and the dark, winding, narrow path through the rock seemed interminably long.

Eventually though, I saw light at the end of the tunnel.

My heartbeat quickened.

We emerged into a much bigger cavern, the narrow river opening out into another pool. But unlike the last pool, this one ran straight over the edge of a sheer drop.

I gaped, my pulse racing even as our boat slowed. I could hear the water crashing down over the rocks, and I had no idea how far the drop over the edge was. The cavern beyond was huge, the ceiling impossibly high and the far wall hard to make out.

I moved my eyes to the prince and saw that he was staring at me.

"What is this place?" I asked him, my voice small against the sound of the water. I was relieved that our boat appeared to be completely stationary now, hovering in the middle of the cavern.

"It is a place I have recently discovered," the Prince answered.

"How is the current not taking us over the edge?" I asked, though as I moved my eyes to the shadows filling the sail, I realized I already knew the answer. His magic was keeping us where we were. Which meant anybody without magic would be carried straight over the cliff.

The boat rocked as the Prince moved, ducking one arm down to scoop up a handful of water from the pool.

I suppressed a squeak of alarm and gripped the sides of the boat with both hands. My eyes moved to the waterfall edge, unbidden.

"Drink," said the Prince, and held out his cupped hand to me.

"What?"

"Drink the water from the pool."

I moved as much as I dared to peer into the pool. The water was bright and clear, the rock visible around the sides until inky darkness replaced it. Distrust flowed through me as looked back at the Prince.

"Why would I drink pool water from underneath a mountain, offered to me by a male who wants me dead?"

His jaw tensed. "I don't want you dead. You know I don't want you dead. We have been over this what seems like a hundred times."

"Oh sure. You only want me dead after I've helped you with some secret task that you won't tell me about."

Anger crossed his features, his bright eyes flashing dark. "I am trying to show you now. Fates help me, if you will not do anything you are told this will take a very long time. Time I do not have."

I stared at him and his proffered hand. "I have to

drink the pool water?"

"If you want to leave this place alive with your friends, then yes. Drink the fucking water."

I leaned forward, ready to take a sip. But as I drew my head close to his large hands, I found myself taking in the rough skin that didn't match the clean nails, the fine white scars under silver rings that no fighter could afford.

The male was an enigma, a contradiction. Desire to know more about him filled me, and I drew back. "I'll get my own," I muttered, before carefully dipping my own hand down into the pool. The boat rocked a little, but I was able to keep enough liquid in my hand to sip from.

It tasted of nothing. Just... water.

I looked at the Prince. "What happens now?"

Slowly, he tipped away the water in his own hand, eyes fixed on mine. There was a look I couldn't decipher in them. Probably irritation.

"You are not a patient human."

"No. I'm not."

"Have you considered practicing it?"

"Patience?"

"Yes."

"I'm not sure it's something you can practice."

"Believe me, it is. You are testing mine."

I stopped myself from rolling my eyes. "And you mine. Why did I have to drink the water?"

"I do not know how long it will take to work on a human," he said.

"How long what will take?"

"The effects of the water." His answer made me uneasy, but before I could demand he tell me more, everything turned green.

I gripped the boat edge, blinking around. The green melted into yellow, bright enough it made my eyes water. "What's happening?"

I looked at the Prince and the yellow morphed into orange. The only things not moving through the painfully bright colors were his eyes. They stayed clear icy blue as the orange faded to red.

"You are receiving the sight."

"What sight? Everything's the wrong color!" Panic laced my words, red turning to purple.

"It will return to normal in a moment."

The idea of everything I could see rolling through the colors of the rainbow permanently made me feel abruptly motion sick. But as everything moved to blue, and much darker, there was a moment of fuzziness that gave me new cause for panic. Just as I began to shake my head blindly, gripping the boat so hard my fingers hurt, everything cleared.

And the cavern didn't look the same as it had before.

All the colors were back to normal, only now, there was something jutting out over the cliff edge.

It was an arm. A giant stone arm, three times as wide as I was, ending in an open hand, palm facing up and hovering over the empty space below. Standing on the palm were statues. I was too far away to make them out clearly, but they were in a ring, facing inward.

"You can see it?"

"If by *it* you mean an enormous stone arm rising out of the water holding a load of statues over a sheer drop, then yes. I see it."

"Good."

The boat began to move, and I shook my head slowly as it butted gently against the stone wrist.

"I'm not getting out of this boat."

"Yes. You are."

The Prince moved easily from the little vessel onto the part of the stone arm that rose from the water. He held his hand out to me.

"No."

"You are scared?"

I blinked at him. *Yes.* But how the hell was I supposed to admit that to him? "No."

"Then why will you not come?"

I glared at him. He knew full well I was scared. Defiance soared through my veins, replacing the fear. I slapped his hand out of the way and scrambled out of the boat, getting my backside on the stone before slowly standing up. The wrist was wide, and I felt sturdier on the makeshift bridge than I thought I would.

"Good." The Prince turned and strode down the arm, only pausing when he reached the cliff edge. He looked over the side, glanced back at me, then continued until he reached the palm and the ring of statues.

You've got this, Reyna. This is what you need. Find out what he wants. Get leverage. Do as you're told. Don't fall over a waterfall under a mountain and die.

I took a deep breath and followed him.

CHAPTER 22

I elected not to look over the edge when I passed the waterfall. Instead, I kept my eyes firmly forward, refusing also to look at the Prince. I picked the back of the closest statue and concentrated hard, putting one foot in front of the other with a confidence made from nothing but adrenaline.

When I made it to the statues, I reached out, gripping the arm of the one I'd been so focused on.

"Thank you," I mouthed to the statue, moving slowly around it to see its face.

I moved my head back in surprise. It had no face. Slowly, I looked around at the others. None of them had faces, the rock missing, as though it had been bashed off.

There were five fae depicted, each holding a staff. As I moved around the ring, I realized that there was one from each Court. I found myself drawn not to their missing faces, but to their staffs. There was a shadow-fae with a skull on his staff, a gold-fae with wings on hers, a male ice-fae, with spikes jutting from his staff, a female fire-fae, her staff made of rock and covered in beautiful curves, like flames, and there was an elderly earth-fae, his staff made from gnarled wood and covered in tiny delicate leaves.

There were three more statues with no staffs, and I reached up, brushing my fingers over the tops of their empty hands, where their staffs should be. One of the three statues was taller than the others, and one much shorter. Other than their height, it was hard to distinguish anything else. All of the statues were made from the same pale stone as the ones inside the trunk of *Yggdrasil* had been.

I looked at the Prince, who was watching me closely. "Who are they?"

"Fae."

"And the three with no staffs?"

"I don't know. I was hoping you would."

I frowned at him. "Why?"

He pointed to the center of the palm. A small, circular indent caught my eye, and I moved, crouching to see it better.

There was an inscription in the ancient language. My heart thudded hard in my chest.

The copper-haired gold-giver has the key.

I looked back up at the Prince, masking my features.

In the Gold Court, knowing the ancient language was a weapon. If the fae didn't know you understood it, they would use it around you, revealing things they would otherwise keep hidden. Making a quick decision to employ the same tactic in the Shadow Court, I shrugged my shoulders.

"What does it say?" I asked.

The Prince's eyes narrowed. "You do not speak the language?"

"No."

"It says that the copper-haired gold-giver has the key."

It wasn't too difficult to feign my confused reaction. "What key?"

"You tell me. That is why I have brought you here."

"Where is here? Who put this here? What is it?"

"I have my suspicions. But until you prove yourself trustworthy, I have no intention of sharing them with you."

"You think I'm the untrustworthy one?" To be fair, he was right not to trust me. But that didn't stop me defending my honor.

"Yes. Half the words that leave your lips are lies."

"Only to you," I said, before I could stop myself. His lips twitched, I guessed in annoyance.

"What is the key?" he asked me.

I raised my hands, staring at him. "I have no idea. I have no idea what any of this is."

"Then look." He gestured at the statues.

I turned in a slow circle. "I am looking. I have no idea what this is."

"Look harder." There was frustration in his tone. I sought the gold-fae statue, trying to slow the questions in my head.

Was I really the copper-haired *gold-giver* the inscription was referring to? Confusion welled through me. How could something that felt as ancient as these statues have a reference to me?

Voror's words came to me, as I touched the cool stone of the female gold-fae's face. He had been instructed to help the copper-haired gold-giver.

Well, there was no point fighting it. Someone, somewhere, had a plan for me.

I switched my gaze from the fae's face to her staff. It was as nice as anything I had ever made. If it wasn't made of stone, then it would be beautiful. Even as I thought the words, something glinted, catching my eye.

One of the feathers in the left wing over the top of the staff was crooked. How had it glinted, though? I leaned closer, then took in a sharp breath as a golden rune floated into being.

"There's gold here," I whispered, feeling its power.

"There is?"

The Prince was by my side in seconds, and I pulled away as his scent washed over me. "Yes. Will you back up? I need space."

He took a step away, his presence still looming. I leaned close to the statue again, brushing my fingers over the stone wings. Heat tingled through my fingertips. Carefully, I picked at the stone with my nail. A tiny bit crumbled away, and I bit my lip.

Gold.

I heard an intake of breath behind me, but I didn't

turn. Precisely and slowly, I scratched away another little bit of stone, revealing more gleaming gold.

"I need tools," I said. "I risk damaging the gold otherwise."

"I do not care if the gold is damaged. I need you to find the key."

I turned to him. "I have no idea what the key is. But I do know that these statues are old, and I wouldn't want to risk damaging anything on them." My affinity with the precious metal made me fiercely protective of it, but that wouldn't matter to him. I had to word my request carefully. "The inscription told you I had the key. If you need my help, then you need to let me work as I am supposed to." *And let me buy time.*

His bright eyes bored into mine, and I held his gaze. "Fine. We will return, with tools."

Without another word, he swept around and began striding back along the wrist, toward the boat.

I looked back at the gold inside the statue. What was it doing under the palace of the Shadow Court? I looked at the other statues. Would a *flame-forger* find fire inside that staff? Or a *water-winder* find liquid in the ice-fae statue?

I moved to the wrist, and at the return angle it was impossible not to look at the crashing water falling over the edge of the cliff. My eyes automatically moved down, to see where the fall ended, but I snapped them closed before they could. When I opened them again, I made sure I was looking dead ahead. Fixing my focus on the figure of the Prince standing at the end, I made my careful way across the arm.

We were both silent in the boat on the way back through the narrow passage. It seemed the longer I spent in this world, the more questions I had, and fewer answers.

There was something about the statues. A power and an age that spoke to me on a level only gold did. They were important, that much I was sure of. If they held a power that could be accessed by the fae then I could see why the Prince wanted it unlocked. And I could only imagine what his stepmother might do with it.

Of course, they may just have been statues. They looked and felt like smaller versions of the ones inside the trunk of *Yggdrasil*, and whilst those ones undeniably held power, they didn't provide miracle access to something that could change the world. So why did it feel like these smaller statues were more important?

And why were they hidden in a pool under a mountain in the Shadow Court, invisible until revealed, and dangerously accessible over the edge of a cliff?

"How did you know to drink the water?"

We had reached the first cavern with the door back to the palace, and were climbing out of the boat onto the small beach.

The Prince glanced at me. "I will tell you when you have made some progress."

I screwed my face up, but said nothing. It was as I expected. And he had already taken a risk showing me something so secret.

It didn't matter to me how he found the statues. All that mattered was escaping. *And finding out why an ancient inscription refers to you, and finding the fae who sent a crazy owl to help you.*

I cursed the thought as it intruded. Escaping and keeping Lhoris and Kara alive was the goal. Not finding out who I was. Or why I had been sucked into a world, and a mystery, I had no idea I was a part of.

I was starting to worry I wouldn't be able to do one without the other, though.

The Prince's shadows swirled, and the door in the stone swung open. Before he stepped through, he fixed his gaze on me. In the low light his face looked rougher. Meaner. "I will not hesitate to kill your friends if you breathe one word of the shrine to any other living soul."

Magic accompanied his threat, tingling and cool as the shadows swirled about us.

I nodded. "I understand,"

"Good. Return to your room and make me a list of the tools you require. I will source them immediately."

I was splashing water on my face in my bathing chamber when I heard the fluttering of wings.

I peered around the door.

Voror was perched on the corner of the bedpost, blinking around the room.

"Good morning," I said to the owl.

"It is not especially. I abhor daylight hours." He blinked, managing to convey his annoyance in the slow motion. "But since humans do most of their business during the day, and I have been ascribed to help a human, here I am."

"I see."

"Have you learned anything new?"

The Prince's threat loomed at the back of my mind. Technically, Voror was a living soul, so telling him about the shrine went against his instructions. But Voror had been told to seek me out by someone who must already know something about all of this.

"Do you know anything about ancient statues? Or me being the key to something?"

The owl tilted his head slowly. "No. Why?"

I told him about the cavern and the statues. "The Prince called it the 'shrine', and word seems pretty fitting," I finished.

"I would like to see this place."

"You can't when the Prince is there. And without his magic there's no door, and no way to stop the boat going straight over the edge of the waterfall."

"Hmm. I will ponder this."

"You do that."

A knock on the door made him beat his wings in surprise.

"I thought you were a superior predator, did you not hear them coming?" I teased him.

He clicked his beak as he took off for the window. "It is obviously someone of equal stealth and might."

"My lady? It's me, Brynja," my maid called through the door.

I couldn't help the smirk I gave Voror. "My slight, and buxom, handmaid," I told him.

Voror ruffled his feathers as he landed on the windowsill. "I must be feeling the adverse effects of being out in the day. I will return at dusk."

"Isn't it always dusk in this place?" I looked past him at the gloomy sky.

"Absolutely not. Your pathetic human eyes may not be able to tell, but mine are—"

"My lady? Is everything okay?" the maid knocked again, interrupting him.

"Yes, just a minute," I called back. "We are returning to the shrine today, so try to come back soon," I said to Voror. If there was any way of him following us, I wanted to find out. After all, he could fly through rock.

Voror gave a soft hoot, which I took as agreement, then flew through the pane of glass.

I opened the door to Brynja's concerned face. "My lady, you have been summoned. I don't have long to get you ready."

"Summoned?"

"Yes. In place of last night's dinner, the Queen wants to have lunch with you. Now."

CHAPTER 23

I expected the queen's dining hall to be as unpleasant, dark, and filled with blood and bones as the throne room had been. It did have the maroon, blood-colored walls, and there were bones everywhere, but in a starkly different way. There were no decaying bodies hanging from the ceiling, but there were six grand chandeliers made from skulls. They increased in size as they dropped, tiny animal ones at the top, and ending with human looking ones. Candles flickered inside the mouths, casting shadows over the table below, which was carved from very dark wood and set magnificently with black crockery and fine green-tinged glassware.

Huge arch-shaped windows dominated one wall of the room, spanning from the floor to the ceiling. So far, they had been the only thing that reminded me of the Gold Court palace; except the view from these ones showed no bright, golden warmth. They showed a velvet blanket, pinpricked with stars, over the sparkling lights and motion of the towns dotting the mountain side below.

The opposite wall held a dresser built into the space, probably twenty feet long. At intervals there were decanters filled with liquids of varying colors, and the odd statue of a snake or raven.

The Queen sat at the head of the table, and the sight of her made my skin prickle and feel inexplicably too tight for my body.

She was dressed similarly to when I'd last seen her, in a tight black gown. Her hair was up in an equally elaborate style. The only obvious difference was the absence of blood trickling down her cheeks.

"My son. Peculiar little *gold-giver*," she acknowledged us as we entered. A human thrall, dressed in a thin black robe that left little to the imagination, immediately darted forward, pulling out a chair on her left. I looked at the Prince, and he nodded at the chair, indicating I was to go in that direction.

"Where is Rangvald?" he asked as he went to the other side of the table, taking the seat opposite mine. The wood of the chair was the same as the table, dark and rich, and the upholstered seat had a pattern made up of intertwined snakes. I sat, trying to keep my heightening nerves at bay.

The Queen's predatory gaze roved over me, and I found myself distinctly grateful for the headband the

Prince had warded. It felt warm on my head, as though reminding me of its presence.

"He will be here shortly." She gave me a strange smile, her black eyes hard to read. "How was your first night in our home?"

"Very comfortable. Thank you."

I glanced at the Prince long enough to see a tiny flicker of relief on his face.

"If you are comfortable, then my son is not doing his job properly." She looked at him. "Mazrith? Why have you allowed this little tool of our enemies comfort?"

I couldn't help my intake of breath when I looked at the Prince.

His face had changed completely. The rough warrior was gone, and the beautiful fae was beaming through instead. Promise filled his eyes as his lips turned up in a sinful smile. When he spoke, seduction laced his tone.

"You will not be so comfortable tomorrow, my little *gildi*."

He had just called me his little feast.

My heart hammered in my chest, and I tried to take my eyes from his beautiful, compelling, desire-filled face.

I opened my mouth to tell him he could feast elsewhere, but all that came out was a slow breath.

This was an act. An act for his stepmother.

And I wasn't supposed to understand the language.

The Queen gave an unpleasantly high-pitched laugh. "My son, I don't know how much fight you'll get from this one. She seems rather slow."

The doors at the end of the room burst open and the man from the day before with the balding head and silver slippers strode into the room, bowing low. "My Queen, forgive my tardiness. I am, as ever, at your disposal."

He moved to my side of the table, and with a sinking feeling, I realized he was headed for the chair next to mine. "And a good day to you. Reyna, is it?"

I nodded, but stayed silent. He clapped his hands as he sat down, and a stream of thralls entered the room, carrying trays. They were set down in an efficient parade, clearly well practiced. Plates were placed in front of each of us, all covered with a silver cloche.

Apprehension skittered through my gut, the thought of the bodies on the ceiling from yesterday filling my head. What would be under the dome covering the plate? I looked sideways at the Queen, my nerves increasing as I saw the delighted stare she was giving me.

I held my breath as the human slaves moved behind each of us, reaching over to grip the cloches. As one, they lifted the domes, then disappeared from the room.

I stared down at my plate. There were two pale cuts of meat and piles of delicately arranged vegetables in colors I had never seen in food. I poked at something bright orange.

"It's a carrot," the Queen said slowly. "You have never seen a carrot?"

I shook my head, cheeks burning at how stupid she was making me feel. Cruel amusement shone in her face, and she reached over to my plate, lifting the slices of orange vegetable from them with her fingers.

"Really, you have picked a fine wife here," she said sarcastically, turning to Mazrith and holding up the carrot. "Is she mute?"

"Sadly not," he said, with an equally sarcastic smile at me, which quickly turned wolfish, and my face burned even hotter.

"Open your mouth," the Queen said, turning back to me.

"No." The word snapped out. I couldn't have held it back if I'd wanted to.

She pouted at me. "Oh, little girl, you need to do as you are told. If I am to be denied the pleasure of killing you, you must at least let me have a little fun."

Fear made my breath come quicker as she reached to one side with her empty hand and lifted her staff.

My eyes snagged on it, momentarily lifting me from my situation.

It was like no staff I had ever seen.

On the outside, it looked like a shadow staff, a silver skull on the top and a series of snakes writhing over it in an arch. Not too far in design from the Prince's. But there was something about it...

I leaned forward without even realizing I had moved.

Shadows rushed from the end of it, whipping around me and pinning me to the back of the chair. Ice cold tendrils solidified as snakes, and they slithered across my face, making me gasp.

The Prince's voice sounded in my head. *"Let her play with you."*

I paused my struggling long enough to glare at him.

He looked back at me, a bored, imperious expression on his face that didn't match the tightness of his mental voice.

A shadow snake eased its way across my jaw, then pushed at my closed lips.

Panic and nausea combined, and I shook my head hard. Nothing would dislodge the shadows though.

The Queen laughed. "I only want to be a part of such an important experience. Your first carrot. I find trying new things so rewarding."

"Open your accursed mouth and let her do it." This time the Prince's voice was angry, but when I looked at him he was forking a potato into his own mouth, appearing completely indifferent.

A growl in the back of my throat escaped, and the snake forced itself between my lips.

The Queen sprang up from her chair, and the shadows moved, dragging my head back. She dropped the slices of carrot into my open mouth, before my jaw slammed back closed with enough force to make me see stars.

The shadows seeped away. I blinked groggily, pain welling up in the back of my head.

"Don't forget to chew," the Queen said sweetly, sitting down again.

"You know, as my betrothed, it should be me who feeds her," the Prince said mildly.

"I can feed myself," I said, my words slurred. I tried to chew the warm vegetable in my mouth, anger and pain making my face burn.

"Then eat," the Prince said.

The Queen gave me another smile, then turned her attention to her own food.

Silence fell over the room as she tucked in. The Prince gave me a pointed look, and I forced myself to swallow the carrot and scoop up more food. I avoided the meat, deciding not to trust the Queen even an ounce.

"So, how are your plans coming along?" she said to Mazrith eventually. "I can't wait to hear exactly why you need to marry this pathetic human to execute them." Her sickly sweet voice carried an obvious undercurrent of anger.

"I have to wait for Tait to finish his current staff, then he will be assisting us. You will have an update at the end of the week."

I stabbed at something green and bean-shaped a little too hard, my fork scraping on the plate.

"Tell me Reyna, have you ever worked for the Queen of your disgusting Court?" the Queen asked.

I shook my head, feeling myself tense. The Queen of the Gold Court was her sister. "No. I have never worked for her."

It wasn't strictly true. I had repaired a small part of the Queen's staff a few years ago, but I hadn't interacted with her directly for more than a few minutes.

"Do you know if she is healthy?" The question surprised me. I hadn't thought her capable of compassion.

"I believe so, yes."

The Queen's face darkened. "Accursed fucking female."

I went back to my vegetables. Not compassion after all, then.

"And Reyna, how many *gold-givers* did you work with in the palace?" Rangvald's voice was amiable, and I eyed him warily.

"A few."

"How many?"

"Five." There was no point lying to him. They had three of us already. "How many shadow-spinners work in this palace?" I threw the question out with no expectation of an answer. Or, in fact, any real interest in the answer. But when he spoke, my attention moved entirely to him.

"Two."

Only two?

My surprise must have shown on my face, because he gave me a small shrug. "Rare things, the rune-marked." His eyes flicked from the mark on my wrist to the Queen. She had her whole steak impaled on her fork, ripping away lumps with her black teeth like a lion would, a slightly demented look in her eyes.

Fucking crazy didn't come close to what this female was.

"Yes. Rare indeed," the Prince growled. His plate was empty and he rose. "Thank you for the meal. We must get back to our business."

The Queen looked up at him, eyes wide. "Oh no, you must stay. I have dessert. Something Reyna here will love."

I stood up too, doing my very best to keep my expression neutral.

"Food has stirred my... *appetites*. My betrothed and I are leaving. Now." His eyes locked onto me, and his bright blue gaze moved up and down my body in obvious approval.

It wasn't just my cheeks that heated under his gaze. My whole accursed body reacted.

The Queen raised an eyebrow as she sighed. "There is no fighting with a man's desires." She waved a hand. "Dismissed. For now."

Mazrith strode from the room immediately, the doors flying open just before he reached them. I hurried after him, aware of Rangvald's piercing eyes on me the whole time.

As soon as I was sure the door was closed behind us, I spoke. "Just so you know, if you are actually planning to take me to bed—"

He turned to me, cutting my words off. "Your whole world would change in one night. But that is not my plan." His eyes glinted as I swallowed. "I am sick of fighting her. It is easier to play her game, to speak a language she understands."

"You are trying to convince her you took me as your betrothed because you are interested in me..." I trailed off.

"Sexually," he finished for me, and heat flushed every single inch of my body. His eyes flickered down my reddening chest, then darkened. "Yes. I am trying to convince her of that. Do you wish that I was?"

I was saved from answering by the doors slamming open and Rangvald's voice ringing across the hall.

"Prince Mazrith!"

His eyes bore into mine a second longer, then the Prince turned to the slimy fae.

"Rangvald."

"The Queen wishes to extend an invitation to you and your betrothed."

"We are busy."

"Ah, but not too busy to attend your own betrothal ball." He smiled obsequiously, and rubbed his hands together as he looked between us.

"I do not wish for a betrothal ball," the Prince ground out. "But thank her for her thoughtfulness."

"Oh, but it is too late. The arrangements have been made. It begins at midnight."

"Tonight?" The word popped out of my mouth.

Rangvald's lips curled up even higher. "The Queen's Court are more than willing to do as she bids, as quickly as she bids them. And, she wishes to throw her beloved son a party, so that all may see just why he has taken a human thrall as his bound wife." The words hardened, and so did Mazrith's stare. "Members of Court are whispering, Mazrith. You must show them that Reyna here is worthy of a position in our palace."

"I will see you at midnight, then," he growled.

Rangvald dipped his head, then strode back into the dining room, his slippered feet silent on the tiles.

The Prince bared his teeth, then began to ascend the grand staircase.

"How can she plan and throw a ball in one day?" I muttered as I followed him.

"Within these walls she can do as she pleases. She was my father's wife," he spat, before whirling to face me. "She has taken the game a step further. We must play it."

"What do you mean?" I blinked up at him, towering over me on the staircase.

"Prove to the courtiers that I have taken you as an interesting plaything. That I am using you to taunt our enemies."

I bared my teeth. "I am not a fucking toy."

"Have I treated you as one?"

I glared at him.

"You took me from my home and threatened to kill my friends."

"And I have treated you and them with respect since, as I gave my word I would."

He hadn't laid a finger on me, which in itself was strange. All the fae of *Yggdrasil* took whatever they wanted. And the Prince of the Shadow Court was legendary for wanting everything.

"And when you no longer have a use for me?"

He took a step down, level with me, eyes blazing. "You won't get a chance to find out if my stepmother loses patience. As much as I loathe saying it, father's passing left her as the ruler of this Court. Play her fucking game, and you might stay off her ceiling long enough to find out what I'll do with you."

Power thrummed through the air between us, and I

believed him. Both his threat, and what he believed the Queen capable of.

"What do I have to do?"

"Exactly as you're told."

Shit.

CHAPTER 24

"First, we're going to get your tools." He turned, and I felt like I could breathe properly again, the intensity between us lessening as soon as I couldn't see his face.

Frima was waiting at the top of the stairs. The two fae nodded at each other, and then turned off down a hallway.

"Good day to you too," I muttered to the female's back as I hurried after them.

She looked over her shoulder at me with an expression that made me wonder instantly if she knew about last night. Svangrior had said he wouldn't tell the Prince, but he never said anything about the Prince's warriors.

"It is far from a good day," she said.

I kept my lips clamped shut. Staying quiet in the Queen's dining room was easier than biting back retorts to Frima, but I could do with the practice.

The truth was, I was grateful for Frima's presence.

Being alone with the Prince was becoming unnerving for a whole host of reasons other than the fact that he was terrifying.

"Tait is waiting for us," Frima said to the Prince.

"Good. I could do with the ride."

She nodded. "Tell me about it. Can she ride?"

I scowled, instantly losing my resolve to keep my mouth shut. "If by *she*, you mean me, then no. Of course I can't ride," I said. "How many thralls do you think are taught to ride?"

Frima sighed, then fell back a step so that she was in line with me. I looked at her sideways, warily. She began to speak slowly and clearly, as though I were a child. "We are going to the stables, and then onto a small town nearby where Maz's shadow-spinner works. He has many tools in his workshop that Maz tells me you need access to." Her eyes tightened and her voice dropped. "If you make one move to escape, it will not be you that pays the price. Understand?"

She knew about my escape attempt.

I stared back at her, keeping my chin held high. "I have no intention of trying to escape."

She snorted. "Forgive me for being inclined not to believe you."

I shrugged. "What would be the point?" I played on what I knew she would believe. "He would just find me again." I pointed at the Prince's back.

"Hmm. Perhaps you're not as stupid as you've been making out," she said doubtfully.

"You know, I've never been called stupid more than I have in the last few days."

Frima tipped her head. "If enough people are saying it, it must be true."

I glared at her, then flinched as the Prince's voice sounded in my head.

"I do not believe for one moment you are stupid. I am watching you, little gildi.*"*

I was relieved to discover the stables Frima had referred to were not the same stalls I had found myself in the night before.

They were at the bottom of a long spiral staircase that was very similar, but the door at the end of the corridor was carved with horses instead of bears and reptiles. When we entered, I could smell hay, and the light was welcomingly bright. Large torches high on the stone walls held flames big enough to give a warmth to the space that I had not encountered anywhere else in the palace.

The sound of snickering horses and clopping hooves came from behind many short stable doors separating the animals. The Prince moved purposefully on, until a sturdy-looking human man came hurrying out of one of the stalls.

"Your highness, will you be requiring Jarl?"

"Yes. And Idunn."

The man I presumed to be the stable hand looked at me. "And a third horse?"

"No."

"Very good, your highness." The man hurried off again.

When he came back, he was leading a beautiful horse that had been prepped and saddled. Unsurprisingly, she was black. She had purple streaks through her mane and tail, and a single deep grey diamond on her nose. Bright, intelligent eyes blinked at Frima, and she tossed her head when the fae rubbed her long snout.

The stable hand left again, and Frima put one leg in the stirrup, gripped the saddle, and neatly vaulted herself up onto the horse's back, which was easily five feet off the ground.

I wasn't sure I would be able to pull a move like that off, but I would sure as Odin try.

My resolve faltered when the stable hand reappeared, though.

I had never seen a horse like the one he was leading to the Prince. He was breathtaking.

Deep black in color, he had silver bands around the tops of his legs and around his massive, sleek chest. Within the silver strips were runes, hundreds of them, tiny and detailed. The stallion swished his tail, and I noticed silver streaks in the hair, matching the Prince's braids.

The horse danced impatiently, hooves skipping on the stone. The stable hand passed the reins over to the Prince and then backed up a little nervously.

"He doesn't look real," I muttered as the Prince laid a large hand on his flank, and he stilled.

"Oh, he is very, very real. Sometimes a little too real," the stable hand muttered.

Frima gave him a look. "At least he can be ridden. I heard his sister was the cause of two broken arms just last week?"

The stable hand nodded gravely, and the Prince sighed. "Unless you can bring my mother back from the grave, I fear she will stay untameable." He looked at me. "Have you ever been on a horse?"

"No."

"Hold the reins, and do exactly as you're told." He narrowed his eyes. "I haven't got time to fix your body when you fall six feet to the stone. Do as you're told."

I gave him a sarcastic smile. "Yes, your highness."

His face twitched into a scowl, then he moved so quickly I didn't see it coming. I yelped as he wrapped his hands around my waist and lifted me clean off my feet.

He swung me up onto the horse, my legs flailing. I grabbed the reins, gripping the horse's huge back between my thighs. "Some warning would have been nice," I said through gritted teeth, then yelped again as the huge beast moved. "I'm not even in the saddle!" I was in front of the saddle, up by the horse's massive shoulder blades.

In another lightning swift movement, the Prince vaulted into the saddle behind me. His hands were on my waist again, and then I was lifted backward.

Into his lap.

195

I froze.

"I'll take those," he said, his chest rumbling against my back before his arms moved either side of my body and took the reins from my hands. At a small clicking noise from the Prince, the horse began to trot forward. I moved my hands instinctively to the stiff leather of the saddle front, holding on and trying to stop the shake that threatened to take my limbs.

My whole body pressed against his. And it felt... *good*.

Better than good.

I could feel the flex of the muscles in his huge chest as we moved on the horse, feel his powerful thighs around mine. Every part of me wanted to press back, see what else I could feel.

I gave myself the hardest mental slap I was capable of. *This is his power, he's fae royalty. Of course he's attractive!*

But, I hadn't felt a man against me in a long time, and my body was reacting without my permission. And even when I *had* been this physically close to a man, I couldn't recall feeling so...ignited. I felt like someone was holding a torch under my skin, creating bolts of tingling heat that travelled straight to my core.

"Relax. If you stay this stiff, then you'll fall." The Prince's quiet voice made me start.

"I can't relax. I'm in your lap," I hissed back.

I felt him move back a little and I slid down him, my backside meeting the leather of the saddle. My heart hammered in my chest. Had I just felt what I thought I'd felt?

I was pinned between him and the saddle front, and every inch of his body was still pressed against mine.

"Better?" he asked.

"No," I said, and my voice was a breathy croak.

"Well, I'm comfortable." His arms closed around me as he moved the reins, and he made another clicking sound. I gasped as the horse took off, cantering out of the stables.

I gaped around, clinging to the saddle as I bounced against the Prince. We were in a forest, trees stretching high into the gloomy sky. They were formed out of the strangest shapes I had ever seen. One looked like it was made of people, all of them twisted together in agony and another looked like it had been struck by lightning, its branches a tangle of its charred remains.

We picked up speed, making it harder to see anything clearly. The wind blowing through my hair was cool, and welcome on my hot face, and I tried to let myself feel the movement of the horse instead of the Prince behind me. The more ground we covered, hooves hammering the hard soil, the easier it became to fall into a rhythm. By the time we burst out of the trees, the stiffness had left my limbs, and I only realized when we slowed down that I had begun moving against the Prince with the gait of the horse.

I had never imagined the feeling of sheer freedom being on the back of the beast would give, and my cheeks were flushed with exhilaration, rather than embarrassment. Was riding always like this?

"He likes you."

I almost turned at the Prince's unexpected words, but Frima called out. "I'll go ahead."

She galloped off, along the stone cobbled path we had reached. Ahead of us were buildings, all made from dark wood or grey stone. Light filled every window, and I could see why the towns sparkled from a distance. Everything looked warmer and somehow more inviting than such a dark place should.

"This looks friendlier than the forest," I said, as the horse ambled slowly along the path and into the town. I tried to ignore the way my backside was rocking into the Prince.

"The forests surrounding the palace are not safe," he said.

"And the towns are?"

"Not for you."

I was about to ask about raids, but the sight of an alehouse made me pause. There was uproarious laughter coming from inside and singing. Golden light streamed from the windows, and a wave of something that might have been jealousy washed over me.

To live a normal life. It was beyond anything I could ever hope for.

"My shadow-spinner should have the tools you need. Be quick in gathering them." The Prince drew my attention back to him.

"Why does he have tools? Surely spinning shadows doesn't need equipment?"

I felt a rumble in the prince's chest. "Wrong. Shadow spinning requires its own tools. And he is somewhat eccentric."

"Why doesn't he live in the palace?"

"Because he lives here."

"That's not an answer. I meant, why don't you keep him in the palace where you can keep him safe? Especially if the palace only has two of them."

"He is safe here."

We turned down a small alleyway, and I saw Frima's horse tied up outside a large stone building with a massive chimney on one side.

We dismounted, the Prince lifting me from the saddle. For a beat, I felt unsteady and reached out without thinking, laying my hand on the horse's massive flank to right myself.

The horse snorted loudly, and flicked his tail.

"Easy, Jarl," the Prince soothed, before sliding gracefully out of the saddle.

I took a slow step back, hands held up submissively as I stared at the horse. "Thanks for the ride," I whispered. "It was amazing." Jarl's black eye found mine, and his tail stopped swishing.

The door to the building flew open, and a small, human man with a shock of grey hair beamed at us. "Your highness," he said to the Prince, then nodded at me. "Welcome to the workshop."

CHAPTER 25

When I stepped into the workshop, I drew in a breath of surprise.

Tait was the Prince's shadow-spinner, and whilst I had no idea how, exactly, shadows were spun, I was pretty sure he didn't need the vast array of items I could see.

There were urns and mirrors and statues, clocks and candlesticks, bottles and jars filled with powders and liquids, items I didn't even recognize, all covering every available surface. The room was filled with tables, each piled high with objects, and shelves lined the walls, all just as full.

Even the ceiling was covered in items, bells and tankards and decorative wooden ornaments hanging from the rafters.

In the center of the room was a machine made from black metal that looked a little like a sewing spindle. Surrounding it were needles that looked to be made of bone and silver, and a pile of metal rods. *Rods that would become staffs,* I realized.

I stepped toward the spinning machine, and Tait coughed. "We would have to trade secrets, if you wanted to look at that," he said cheerfully.

I looked at him, a flurry of excitement blossoming in my chest. "You would tell me how you spin shadows?"

"Would you tell me how you work gold?"

I hesitated. Before I could work out an answer, the Prince spoke, putting a stop to the fledgling conversation. "We are looking for tools this *gold-giver* might need to perform her work," he said.

"Ah, yes. I should have something somewhere." Tait began to dig around in a pile of stuff on a table near the back, sheets of glimmering blue fabric and streams of fine metal chain falling to the floor as he rummaged.

"Why do you have all this?" I asked, still staring.

Tait shrugged. "Well, mostly, I believe in fate. And the fates have told me I need to be prepared."

"Prepared?"

"Well technically, it's Maz," his cheeks colored a little and he looked at the Prince. "Sorry, *Your Highness*, here who needs to be prepared, not me. But with the Queen and her—."

Frima stood up, cutting him off. "Tools, Tait. Find the tools, and stop talking."

"Yes, yes, of course."

He came over a moment later with a heavy leather roll. When I unwound it, I saw a toolkit almost as good as my own at the palace, scalpels and tweezers and fine engraving points all in amazing condition.

"Where in the name of Odin did you get this?"

"I paid a high price to have it smuggled in," he said proudly. "I have kits for all fae magic."

"But you are enemies with all other fae. Why would you pay for this?" I held up the roll, frowning.

"Know your enemy, girl. That's what they say." He touched the side of his nose knowingly.

"I appreciate your help, Tait," the Prince said, moving to the door.

"Oh, Your Highness, could I, erm, have a word in private, before you go?" The man looked awkwardly between me and Frima.

The female nodded at me, then at the door. "We'll wait outside."

I held up the tool roll. "Thank you," I said.

"You're welcome. Whatever you need them for, I hope they are adequate."

We left the Prince in the workshop, Frima's horse snickering happily when she saw her master, and Jarl eyeing me warily. I looked again at the tool roll. There was a familiarity in it, a soothing feeling from its presence I hadn't known I'd missed.

"You're lucky, you know." Frima's words broke me from my thoughts and blinked at her as she stroked her horse's snout.

"Lucky?"

"Svangrior has a temper on him. But so does Arthur." I held her gaze. "You and your friends could have been killed a number of times last night. And then again this morning, if Maz found out."

"You expected me to do nothing? Accept my kidnapping and stay quiet like a good little girl?"

"No. I'd have done exactly the same thing."

My brows shot up. "You would?"

"Uh-huh. Only I'd have actually escaped." She gave me a grin, then turned to the horse, pushing her face into its neck. The door banged behind us and the Prince strode out, his eyes angry and dark. A thrill of something that was either fear or admiration swirled through me, and I gritted my teeth in annoyance.

"Frima, take her back. I have to check on something."

Frima nodded.

"But—" I started.

"Get ready for the ball. I will collect you in a few hours." He launched himself onto his horse in one smooth movement and took off down the cobbles at a gallop.

The ride back on Frima's horse was as exhilarating as the first one had been, minus the pressure of a huge male against my body.

I fell into the horse's rhythm faster the second time and found myself not wanting the race through the creepy trees to end. When we were flying through air, eating up the ground, I felt free. I wasn't forced to stand still or to stay within walls when I was on the horse's powerful back. I could go anywhere, feel the air flowing around me. It was the closest thing to freedom I had ever felt.

"You could make a good rider," Frima said when we dismounted, handing the reins over to the stablehand when he hurried over. "See you soon, Idunn," she said, kissing the horse on the end of her nose.

"Why are you being nice to me?" I asked her suspiciously.

"I'm not being nice. I'm stating a fact."

"Huh."

We began walking through the stables, back to the palace. "I heard you say thank you for the first time today."

"Well, I had something to be grateful for. Tait was deserving of my gratitude."

She gave me an assessing look. "Where would you have gone?"

"What?"

"If you'd made it out last night. Where would you have gone?"

"Why would I tell you?" I said defensively. Truth was, I had no idea where we would have gone. Finding a way to the root-river was about all I had as a plan.

"Three *gold-givers*, alone in the Shadow Court, with no weapons or magic." She shook her head. "You got a death wish?"

I glared at her as she held the door open for me. "I'm

under the impression that staying here will lead to the same conclusion."

"I don't know why Maz has wanted you for so long, but I'm sure as Odin it wasn't just to kill you." She glanced down at the tool roll in my hands and I could see how much she wanted to ask me about it.

I held it up. "And when I'm done with this? When I've performed my tasks for his highness like a good little human? Then what?"

She looked between my face and the roll. "Maz isn't who you think he is." Her voice was low, and void of her usual mocking tone.

"The whole of *Yggdrasil* knows who the Prince is," I said.

"The whole of *Yggdrasil* is a fucking mess."

"And that makes him a good guy?"

"It makes a woman who believes what she's told, over what she can see, an idiot." She turned away before I could answer. I followed her in silence, her words sinking through my doubts.

The Prince hadn't stacked up so far with any of the stories. I couldn't deny that.

I hadn't been lashed or beaten once. Nor had my friends, or even my maid. He appeared to be polite to his thralls, and his warriors loved him. And more than once, he had referred to his own integrity as something valuable to him. Even if his beliefs were fucked up, integrity was something sorely lacking in the gold-fae I had experience with.

And then there was his face. It didn't match up with

the arrogant, take-what-he-pleased, fae royalty the rumors had projected. Fierce anger and determination dominated his expressions, filled his bright eyes.

Until he did that seduction thing, and then all my doubts bubbled into something entirely different.

I shook my head, trying to clear the memory of being on the horse with him. *Of what I was sure I had felt as I slid down his hard body.*

We had nearly reached the raven room and I gripped the tool roll tighter. I would concentrate on getting through this ball, and then solving the mystery of the statues. Whatever was down there would bring me closer to finding out what was in store for me, and then hopefully what I could do next.

CHAPTER 26

"Svangrior?" The angry fae was striding away from my room as Frima and I approached it. He whirled around at her call, then scowled when he saw me.

"Yes?"

"I thought you were to accompany us into town?"

"I had things to take care of here. Where is Maz?"

She shrugged. "It seems he has things to take care of too."

She fished a key from a pouch on her belt and unlocked the door to my room.

"Be sure to lock it with magic when she is in there," Svangrior said, glaring at me. I glared back at him before stepping into my room. Part of me was nervous that Voror would be there, and the fae might see him. But the room was empty, no large white and gold owl perched anywhere I could see.

"Behave," Frima said, poking her head through the door. "I'll send Brynja along soon."

"Who has a ball at midnight?" I muttered, as Brynja and I devoured the cheese and bread on the tray she'd brought with her. It had taken a few attempts to get the girl to share the food with me, but eventually she had relented. There was far too much for one person, and we were waiting for the seamstress to deliver the dress I was supposed to wear.

"If it was any earlier, the kitchens and the seam-stresses wouldn't have had time to get everything ready." Brynja shuddered. "Freya help anyone who doesn't deliver what the Queen wants."

"Do you know what room the ball will be held in?" I asked, sending a silent prayer that it wouldn't be in that ghastly throne room.

"There's a grand courtyard, in the center of the palace, my lady."

"Outside?" Hope spiked in me, though I wasn't sure why. It wasn't like having no roof meant freedom.

"Yes. I've not been there myself, but I've heard the others talking about it all afternoon."

There was a knock at the door and the maid rushed to answer it. Frima stepped in holding an armful of black fabric. "Your room having to be locked by magic is a pain in my behind," she scowled. "Apparently I'm now doing deliveries."

Brynja took the dress from her. "Thank you, my lady," she said, dipping low for the fae.

As soon as she was gone, the girl laid the dress out on the bed. I stared at it. "Did you say the seamstress made this today?"

Brynja nodded. "Just for you."

I let out a long breath. "Never in a million years did I think I'd wear something like this."

"Let's see how it fits," Brynja said, clapping her hands together.

It took longer than I would have imagined to get the dress and hair and make-up as the maid wanted it. I was putting my trust in her entirely, not even looking at my reflection until she said she was done. I was worried that my nerves would get the better of me if I did.

Tenacity, a smart mouth, and a talent for provoking people into making mistakes, were where I was comfortable. Wearing ballgowns was a far cry from anything I was equipped to deal with.

"Right, I think that's it. Are you ready to see?"

I nodded. The dress made a pretty jangling noise as I stood up from the stool where she'd been pinning Voror's feather into my hair.

With a deep breath, I looked into the full-length mirror inside the wardrobe door.

Freya help me.

I looked... Well, if it weren't for my copper hair, then I would have looked like one of them. The fae.

The dress was made from black velvet and was outrageously revealing. The neckline plunged between my breasts, the fabric only closing at my naval. The fabric at the shoulders was gathered into two metal tubes of fine rings that were colored gold. A black velvet collar fastened around my neck, and a fine web of intricate gold-colored metal draped down from it, covering my bare skin. A matching belt of glittering metal draped over my hips, down to where a long split in the figure-hugging skirt started.

None of the metal was real gold, but they had made it look like it was.

Black and gold.

A *gold-giver*, betrothed to a shadow-fae.

I drew in another breath. My hair looked incredible, curled artfully around the warded headband with what must have been hundreds of small pins, strands left loose in all the right places. The powder on my cheeks and lips made my eyes look even more green than they were.

"What do you think?" Brynja asked nervously.

"You're very talented," I said, unable to tear my eyes from the woman in the mirror.

It wasn't me. I could see my own features, and the reflection moving as I did. But this woman... She was meant for something more than I had ever been.

"There's a cape. To go with the dress."

I forced myself to turn to the maid. "A cape?"

She moved to the bed and picked up a black swath of fabric. She placed the cape over my shoulders, and turned me around in front of the mirror. The shoulders were formed of interlocking golden scales, almost like short feathers, and the back of the cape dipped low, the fabric connected by golden chains that draped right over my rune mark.

"Fit for a Queen, my lady," Brynja breathed.

"A fae queen."

Brynja's eyes met mine in the mirror, and I couldn't decipher her look. Awe? Or fear.

I would have expected to feel uncomfortable with so much bare skin on show. Refuse to wear the outfit, even. But I felt like I was wearing armor. It made no sense to me, how the lack of fabric could feel stronger than plates and leather. But for the first time since my life had turned upside-down, maybe even the first time in my life, I felt like I could command some sort of respect.

And I needed respect here. I needed allies, and I needed information. The girl inside the fierce dress hadn't changed, I realized, touching my copper hair. She would still give her life to free her friends. And risk everything for a shot at freedom.

When the bang on the door came, I assumed it would be the Prince. But Ellisar was on the other side. "Wow. You look like a fae," he said, before flicking his eyes to my hair. "Sort of."

"Is that a compliment?"

"Doesn't matter what I think," he shrugged. "You get

a human escort tonight, just to really get the court talking," he said, before offering me an elbow.

His war paint was precise, and his leathers clean. He was wearing a black shirt that was tight across his bulky chest, and he smelled like soap. "See you later, Brynja," I said over my shoulder.

Ellisar snorted. "No, you won't. Maz is not letting you go back to your room alone looking like that."

I glowered at him. "You've scrubbed up too, I see."

We began walking along the corridor toward the main staircase.

"It's a ball. There will be mead, and wine."

"And you need to be clean for that?"

"Ah, well. You are talking to man of experience when it comes to balls."

I raised my eyebrows. "Enlighten me."

"Women and wine are a great combination. They lose a lot of their inhibitions. Some of the best nights of my life have involved more than one woman, and a great many more than one bottle of wine. However." He held up a knowing finger. "I've found them more inclined to do all sorts of things if you wash it first."

I held up my own hand, before he could clarify what 'it' was. "Not sure that's the useful insight into fae balls that I was looking for," I said.

"Oh. Right. Erm..." He put his hand to his mouth, thinking. "Don't upset the Queen," he said, eventually. We were halfway down the grand central staircase, and I could hear voices and movement in the main entrance hall below.

"The queen already dislikes me."

"Then avoid the queen. Oh, and don't drink the fae wine. Unless you want to wake up with no idea where any of your clothes are, and a really sore——"

"And that's enough of that story." Frima swooped down past us on the stairs, stopping in front of us. She took in my outfit and tipped her head. "Nice."

"You too." She was wearing a black gown trimmed with purple, with a tight corset top and swishy lace-covered skirt.

"Maz wanted me to give you this." She held out her hand. Sitting in the middle of her palm was a ring.

The wavy band was a silver snake, and the reptile's open jaw held a gleaming red ruby.

I picked it up, the implications of the bond washing over me.

I was bound by unbreakable magic to marry the man who had kidnapped me.

I would never be free.

"I thought women loved jewelry," Ellisar frowned. "Why do you look so sad?"

Frima rolled her eyes at him. "Women also like choosing their own husband, *verslingr*," she muttered. She looked back at me. "You need to wear it. For the ball."

I slipped the ring onto my finger. The metal was cold and hard, and it felt wrong on my skin.

I would find a way out.

I had to.

CHAPTER 27

When the entrance hall came into view, I saw streams of fae being shown across the tiles by scantily-clad human thralls. Their outfits were as ostentatious and luxurious as any I had seen in the Gold Court, but darker in tone and decorated with more skulls.

Everyone had a mask on, I realized, as we descended the grand carpeted staircase. I glanced at Frima and Ellisar, who were now both holding masks in their hands. Frima's was the half skull mask I had seen before, and Ellisars was a simple black eye mask.

"Why don't I have a mask?" I hissed.

"You and Maz are the stars, as denoted by your lack of face-covering," Frima said.

As my feet touched the bottom stair, a female in a tight-fitting bodice dress noticed me, and pointed. Within seconds, the entire hall, fae guests and human slaves alike, had stopped what they were doing and were staring at me.

For a fleeting moment, I wanted to turn and run back up the steps. But I swallowed, and forced myself to raise my chin.

The fae were no better than I was.

They were cruel and shallow, and the only thing that separated them from humans was their power, and in turn, their wealth. *Which you give them with your staffs.* I stamped on the guilty voice in my head.

I would not let them think they were better than me.

I strode across the hall, walking with as much confidence as I could, the heels of the elegant black shoes I'd been given clicking loudly on the checkered floor. Murmurs and hushed laughter followed me all the way to the set of doors Ellisar led us to, set into the space under a long balcony and flanked by two impeccably dressed human men.

The doors burst open as we reached them, and my eyes widened.

It was exactly as Brynja had said. A courtyard set within the middle of the palace.

Smooth, black rock rose on all sides, the walls of the towers and peaks of the palace stabbing at the open sky like the spindles I'd seen in the workshop. The space was large, easily holding two hundred fae and slaves. Twinkling lights danced on chains that were strung between the walls, and it was only when I looked closer that I noticed the candles were held in tiny skulls.

The smell of roasting meat and something sweeter

wafted to me, and a calming tune was being played on a harp, though I could see no musicians. The far side of the courtyard was lined with tables covered in platters, and smaller stone pedestals served as tables that folk gathered around. A sizable space in the middle had been left open for dancing, the floor tiled in exactly the same black and white checkerboard as the entrance hall.

A voice boomed out, and my heart rate picked up. "Announcing Reyna Thorvald, the bound betrothed of Prince Mazrith Andask."

Both the music and the chatter died instantly, and every head turned to me. Ellisar slowly removed his arm from mine, as hundreds of masked eyes bored into me, roving over every inch.

It took every ounce of courage I had to stand there and bear their scrutiny.

"*Gildi.*"

I snapped my head to the source of the voice.

Prince Mazrith strode out of the crowd, a wolfish smile on his face. Tonight, he was every inch the fae. His hair was braided back from his handsome face, and the flickering light of the courtyard softened the scars and stubble I knew marked his skin. He was wearing a black shirt made from what looked like silk, and it clung to his muscular chest in a way that made it hard to look elsewhere. Leather trousers and a wide belt, covered in small glinting weapons and his compressed staff, adorned his bottom half.

His bright blue eyes moved up and down my outfit, and if I had been going to give in to my desire to run back up the stairs at any point, it was at the look in his eyes when they met mine again.

The male looked like he wanted to devour me whole.

I swallowed hard, suddenly too hot in the dress that made me look like a warrior queen in heat.

He had warned me of this.

He was going to play the game. Appease the Queen and Court. Act like he wanted me.

But fuck, he was doing a good job of acting.

Desire engulfed his features, his eyelids drooping and his tongue wetting his lips.

"Fae of the Shadow Court!" He whirled, facing the guests. They parted instantly to give the Queen a better view of her stepson. Standing with Rangvald and two finely dressed fae, she was wearing a floor-length black dress, with long sleeves and a transparent lace bodice that went up over her throat. A black gem was set into the middle of her collarbone, glinting when it caught the firelight. Her hair was an elaborate tumble of black curls around her face, and diamonds dotted her brow and cheeks in place of a mask. Her eyes were fixed on me.

"Allow me to introduce you to a most fascinating creature," the Prince called. "A *gold-giver* from the Court of our sworn enemies."

Excited muttering fired around the space at his words.

"In an unexpected, but most welcome turn of events, we are to be married. Let me assure you that this in no way symbolizes a union between our people." Someone said something I didn't catch, and his sharp gaze moved to a point in the crowd. "By people I mean gold-fae. Not human."

I did my best to keep my expression neutral. Defensiveness made me want to tell every accursed person there that I was human and proud, but I kept my lips clamped together as though they were glued.

"As I'm sure you can see, this girl is no ordinary creature. And I plan to exploit her every virtue, whilst depriving her own court of the same."

A cheer went up from the assembled fae. I felt my eyes narrowing, and took a deep breath.

Play the game, Reyna. He didn't ask for this party. This is the work of the Queen.

The music started again, something fast-paced and sultry. Masked couples began to twirl around the dance floor, and the Prince swept toward me.

When I looked left and right, Frima and Ellisar had vanished. He caught me by my waist, pulling me tight against his body.

"Every man here wants to fuck you," he growled.

I froze. "What?"

He moved back, eyes blazing and his grip tightening on my hip. "Are you trying to make my life a living hell?" His lips barely moved as he spoke the words, and from the intensity of his gaze anyone looking on would have thought he was threatening to take me himself.

There and then.

"This is the dress delivered to my room, by Frima. How, exactly, does anyone else wanting to fuck me make your life difficult?" I tried to keep my own expression sexier than my hissed words.

Light flared in his eyes, followed by drifting shade. "I must claim you as my own."

I couldn't help my scowl. "I'm bound to you." I raised my wrist. "You see what you've done to me?" Rage was building in place of the nerves. "What the fuck else do you think you need to do to mark me as your own?"

He stared at me a beat, then bared his teeth with a snarl. "We dance."

"What?"

He took my hand roughly, pulling me into him. "We dance."

CHAPTER 28

I tried to pull away, but instead, I found myself in his arms, my back against his chest and his arm wrapped around my waist possessively. His other hand held mine up in a tight grip, fingers interlaced with my own, and with a forceful step forward, we began to dance.

The music was slow, sensual, and he guided me through the moves seamlessly. The fae royalty knew how to dance, of course. But the intense warrior I saw in him surely couldn't move like this?

He spun me round and round, and I watched as he turned on his own heel, never losing his grip on my hand. His monstrously tall height should have caused me to stumble, but I remained perfectly balanced in his grip.

I didn't dance.

When would a human slave ever get a chance to dance, besides the drunk chanting in the alehouse? But our bodies played off each other, the sheer closeness...I couldn't help but move with him. He twirled me into his shoulder, and I looked up, eyes tracing over his face, the high curve of his cheekbones, his full, lush lips, and into swirling ice-blue eyes.

I needed to snap out of it. "Are you making enough of a show for you guests?" I choked out, groping for my anger. Trying to force out my increasing physical desire for the monster who had kidnapped me.

"Not yet," he growled, then twirled my body out onto the dance floor. For a second, he was engulfed by the crowd of fae on the dancefloor, then he was tugging me back to him, wrapping a strong arm around my middle as he materialized.

The flat of his palm slid over my hip, down my thigh.

My breath caught.

"I'm human. They'll never believe you chose me because you wanted me," I snarled, digging my fingers into his arm and fighting the urge to arch into his warmth.

"Then make them believe," he said. His lips brushed over my cheek, leaving a burning trail of heat that set every nerve ending in my body afire.

Panic swamped me at the strength of my reaction.

"I hate you," I hissed, channeling all my rushing energy into trying to quell whatever the fuck my body was doing to me.

"Then make them believe it. Wasn't it you who recently reminded me of my reputation? The cruel Prince who would bind a tool of the Gold Court to him in marriage, just to fuck with his enemy." His eyes flared. "The kind of monster who would force a female who hates him to want him."

Anger powered through me, and control over my body flooded back. I moved, separating our bodies, but his grip on my hand was vice-like. "You're twisted," I snarled through gritted teeth.

"And you're a liar."

"What?" He spun me again, tugging me into his side and dipping his head. His lips brushed my ear.

"Tell me, *gildi*, what have you seen in your few short days here with me?" I faltered, not answering him fast enough. "Have I given you a single reason to believe my reasons for binding you to me in marriage were anything other than to save your life?"

Heat was coursing through me, making it hard to think straight. How was he doing this to me?

"You just want me for the statues," I spluttered.

He wanted me for the statues. Just the statues.

He shifted, turning me so that my back was to his chest, and pressed his hand to my stomach. Pressing me back into his body. "You feel that, *gildi*?"

I gulped down air.

I felt it. I felt him. Hard and huge and un-fucking-questionable.

Warm breath tickled my neck as he bent low, brushing his lips across my bare shoulder. "I want you for so much more than what you can do with gold. But you will believe whatever you want to believe."

"Mazrith!" I never thought I would be relieved to hear the Queen's shrill voice. I expected the Prince to release me, but he pulled me tighter. Tighter into the outrageously distracting erection he was pressing into the small of my back.

"I am dancing with my betrothed," he said, the crowds parting in a wide circle around us.

"So I see." She cast a long glance up and down my body, and I wished my cheeks weren't as flushed as I knew they were. "That's quite a dress."

I dipped my head an inch, too distracted by the tower of solid male behind me to remember what I was supposed to do in front of the Queen.

Rangvald coughed next to her. "It does not hold a candle to yours, my Queen," he said.

"Oh, right, no," I said quickly. "Yours is, erm... very regal."

Mazrith's grip somehow tightened even further, and I let out an awkward cough.

"This farce will not be allowed to continue," the Queen hissed suddenly, stepping forward. Her black teeth were bared, and there was a manic glint in her eye. "You are human. A slave. Born of my sister's disgusting Court."

I felt no need to defend the Gold Court, but a surge of defiance for my race rose in me.

Mazrith spoke before I could. "Stepmother, I have given you my reasons for this betrothal," he said so quietly no one else around us would hear. "This little woman will help me in furthering a potentially powerful

223

weapon. And in the meantime, I find myself taken with her uniqueness." He traced a feather-light finger along the ridge of my bare shoulder as he spoke. "She is really very different to any delicacy I've tasted before."

My insides clenched at his words. To be tasted by him would be...

"Mazrith, I do not trust you." Her tone was light, yet the words dripped with venom. "If you are not able to prove to me what purpose she has to you by the end of the week, I want her on my table."

"Table?" The word left my lips unbidden, and her vicious gaze raked over my face.

"My dear, I believe Mazrith to be correct on that front. You will taste nothing like any delicacy I have tried to date."

I recoiled, with nowhere to go but tighter into the Prince's chest.

"Thank you for the party, stepmother," the Prince said. The growl I felt under his clothes didn't match the politeness of his tone.

She stared at him long enough to make me want to be anywhere else, then turned slowly on her insanely high heels and wafted away. Fae fell into step around her, all talking at once, passing her drinks and plates of food that she picked from as she made her way to the doors.

"Is she leaving?"

The Prince lifted my now sweating hand, turning me sharply to face him.

I did everything I could to keep my face neutral and failed.

He was stunning. Light played against every shadow, lifting the pale white scars, highlighting the perfection of his bone structure.

The fae, and the warrior.

The beautiful monster.

"You believe me to be the villain of your story. You are wrong." I watched his lips move as he said the words.

"If she is the villain, what are you?"

He splayed his fingers across my back, and slowly tipped me back, in time with a swooping beat in the music.

His head bent low, tantalizingly close to mine.

"I am no hero." His breath whispered across my lips, his mouth was so near mine.

"I don't need a hero."

"What do you need, *gildi*?"

"Why would I tell you?" My words were a gasp.

He scooped me back up, lifting me clean off my feet as he turned me, then gripping my thigh and lifting my leg as he set me back down. Instinctively, I wrapped my calf around his massive thigh. My core pressed against solid muscle, and I wanted to move against him so badly it almost made me turn and run.

"You would tell me because I am the first person you have ever met in your life that doesn't bore you to fucking tears," he murmured, staring down into my eyes. "Keep that wicked, lying tongue still. I know it is true. I see it in you. You were born for more than your life has offered you. And you know it."

Fear forced its way through the accursed fucking arousal he was causing.

Had he got in my head?

No. He was using a line he likely used on all women. A line that made *him* sound special. Not me.

But fuck, he was right.

I had always known I wasn't meant to spend my life in that workshop. That I had never fit in.

Reyna, that's not exactly hard to work out! You're a slave, with hair nobody else in the five Courts has! I chastised myself, even as his gaze bore into mine.

"And you? What do you want?"

"Right now? You."

His hand slid down my leg, whilst the other snaked up my neck. "I thought we were playing your stepmother's game?"

"Not anymore. She gave us an ultimatum, remember?"

I tried to pull my leg away, but his huge hands tightened.

"Let me go."

His grip loosened instantly. I stepped backwards, and a man dressed in a tiny strip of fabric appeared out of nowhere. He raised a tray covered in glasses of something with bubbles in it, and I swiped one up.

When I looked back at him, the Prince's eyes were loaded with need.

Need he wasn't faking.

"I will fight you," I whispered.

"I will wait."

"What?"

"That wine is dangerous to humans."

I glanced at my glass, and when I looked up he was gone.

CHAPTER 29

For a moment, all I felt was panic at being left alone. Eyes were on me everywhere I looked, and I started to move from the dancing area, headed for a shady spot near a wall where I could hopefully stay unnoticed whilst I worked out what the hell was wrong with me.

"My lady," came Rangvald's quiet voice, as soft fingers touched my arm.

I turned reluctantly. "Good evening."

He eyed my glass. "You know, fae wine is a little strong for humans."

Defiance got through before common sense, and I raised the glass to my lips and took a long swig. It tasted like strawberries, a delight I had only ever savored once before. "Lovely," I said, locking my eyes on Rangvald and channeling as much 'fuck off' vibe as I could his way.

"May I have this dance?" He held out a hand. No

scars or callouses, and perfectly manicured nails, I noted. This man was no fighter.

I didn't want to dance with him. "Actually, I was looking for the—"

He cut me off. "One dance, my lady. I'll make it worth your while."

I frowned. "Worth my while?"

He proffered his hand again, and hesitantly, I took it. He stepped close to me, resting his other hand on my hip. I clamped my own over it and moved it up to my waist.

The hundreds of eyes on me hadn't shifted, and I heard muttering under the soft notes of the piano tune playing.

"My lady, I think you should be aware of something."

His breath was warm on my cheek, and I forced myself not to recoil. There was something about this male that made my skin crawl. Not outright cruelty, like Lord Orm gave off in spades, or twisted mania like the Queen possessed. Just something unnerving.

"There are probably lots of things I should be aware of, Rangvald," I said as politely as I could manage.

He gave a soft chuckle as he moved me in a slow circle. "Let's start with what you already know then. The Queen wishes you dead."

"Yes, I think that's pretty clear."

"You are no ordinary human."

"I am rune-marked," I said slowly.

"Let me rephrase, then. You are no ordinary rune-marked."

My heart skipped a beat. "Why do you say that?"

His dark eyes glinted. "Look at your hair. It is most unusual."

I let out a discreet breath. "Indeed."

"What does the Prince really want with you?"

Ah. Here was the real reason he was talking to me. *Play the game, Reyna.* "You heard him. To make a point to the Gold Court that he stole a valuable asset. And it seems he's quite taken with my hair, too."

The fae smiled at me, a cold expression that held no sincerity. "The Queen has a problem." His voice had dipped low, almost too low for me to hear. "Her tastes are both insatiable and unpredictable."

"Well, she'll have to find a way to satisfy them without me. You heard the prince."

"It is not you I am referring to. There is a reason we only have two *shadow-spinners* left at Court."

My brows drew together. "She's... she's been killing your rune-marked?"

His expression stayed neutral as we continued our slow circle. "Not deliberately. But my lady, I need to know. Has the Prince found a way of helping us?" His eyes darted to the black rune on my hand, and understanding clicked into place.

He thought the Prince was trying to turn me into a *shadow-spinner*.

I eyed him, thinking fast. Rangvald was the Queen's closest ally. And if he thought I could be useful to him and the Court, surely I had a better chance of surviving the Queen's 'insatiable and unpredictable tastes?

"I can't tell you what the Prince is working on," I said evasively.

Rangvald's eyes sparked. "But he is working on something?"

"It is a conversation you should have with him."

"I will, my lady. Thank you." He dipped his head, then fixed his sights on something over my shoulder. "And thank you for the dance. It appears her highness requires me now."

I turned and watched him stride toward the Queen, who was on the far side of the courtyard and had a woman bent double before her.

Turning away again before I could see any more, I found myself taking another glug of the delicious strawberry wine.

"You know you really should be careful with fae wine." Voror's voice sounded in my head, and it made me smile. At least I had one real ally here.

I glanced surreptitiously upward, looking for the owl, but could see nothing.

"I am a master of stealth. You will not spot me."

Unable to answer and taking his words as a challenge, I moved to a vacant spot along the edge of the courtyard and leaned back against the smooth dark stone. Under the pretense of taking in the dancing lights and twinkling windows dotting the rising towers, I scanned the walls for any sign of the white owl.

After a moment, I thought I saw the tiniest flutter of white on a dark window-ledge thirty feet up on my right. I grinned.

"You only found me because I gave you a clue. I felt sorry for your pathetic human eyes."

I shook my head and rolled my *pathetic human eyes*, wishing I could retort.

"Mazrith has left, somewhat early." Frima was walking toward me, skirt swishing. "He said you should get some rest, as you'll be working all day tomorrow."

"Gladly," I said.

She looked at my glass. "You'll sleep well if you finish that. Though Odin knows what kind of dreams you'll have."

"Nightmares?" I asked, then cursed myself for how fearful the blurted word had sounded.

Frima smiled. "Oh no. Fae wine is an aphrodisiac." She jabbed a thumb over her shoulder at the packed courtyard. "Most of the Court will be up til dawn fucking."

"Oh." I felt heat prickle my cheeks.

Frima cocked her head. "With a mouth like yours, I didn't have you down as a prude."

"I'm not a prude," I said, shaking my head. "I just don't feel the need to talk about it."

"Right. You lived with an old man and a girl you treat like a child," she said, nodding. "That's why you don't want to talk about it."

I shook my head again. "Can we go?"

"Sure. You going to bring the wine with you?"

. . .

I followed Frima through the courtyard, aware of all the eyes on me. I pushed my shoulders back and held my chin high, letting the dress do the work it had clearly been designed to do.

I wondered if the seamstress had designed it, or if someone had told her what to do. Certainly not Mazrith, judging from his reaction to it.

Our conversation hurtled through my head in snatches, the intensity of the dance making it hard to recall all of it in order.

"I am no hero."

That was what he had said.

I knew that. Of course, I knew that. But could there be any chance he wasn't the villain either?

After just a few days in the Shadow Court I knew he was starkly different from his stepmother.

But was a few days enough to dispel decades of rumors? They said he forced his enemies to kill their own families, then rot with the bodies. Countless humans and enemy fae had died at his hand. He had kidnapped *me*. Threatened to cut Kara's throat.

In what world did he not play the villain?

We started up the staircase and I tried to pay more attention to the route. Not that I figured I'd get another chance to escape, but it couldn't hurt to be prepared.

"What time is it?" I asked Frima.

"Two hours after midnight. Maz asked for your breakfast to be given at seven."

ELIZA RAINE

I groaned. I had five hours to get some sleep, and my head felt like a hundred loud and needy dogs were rampaging through it.

Frima chuckled. "Drink the rest of the wine. You're human, it'll knock you out cold."

"You think I want to be that vulnerable in this place?"

She gave me a look. "Your room is locked by magic. And if Maz was going to pay you a visit, he'd want you conscious."

"I'll fight you."

"I'll wait."

The words swam back to me, along the way he'd released his grip on me the second I'd told him to.

Fates, the Prince was almost as accursedly confusing as those infernal statues.

We reached the raven room, and Frima paused at the door. "The thralls are all busy downstairs, so no maid."

"Fine," I said, desperate to be alone and not caring one jot that Brynja wasn't there. I pulled the ruby ring from my finger, setting it down on the nightstand. It was a relief to take it off.

Frima looked pointedly at my dress. "You, erm, need a hand getting out of that thing?" My eyes narrowed suspiciously, and she put a hand on her hip, rolling her eyes. "Look, I get it."

"Get what?"

"I'd be doing pretty much everything you are, in your situation."

234

I said nothing, totally unwilling to trust her.

"I'm a lot older than you, Reyna." Her voice softened. "I know something of love. And hate."

I didn't want a speech from her. I had enough to sieve through in my brain, and I didn't believe for one second that could ever be an ally of mine when she was so close to the Prince. "I'm tired."

"And angry, and confused, no doubt."

"This isn't going to work," I said.

She removed her eyemask. "What do you think I'm trying to do?"

"I'm not sure. Either find out what Maz is using me for, because he's not told you, or get me on your side, so I'm easier to control."

To my surprise, she smiled. "Maybe Maz isn't as batshit crazy as I thought he was."

"So I'm right?"

"No. I'm just offering to undo the collar on that dress for you. Nothing more, nothing less."

"Horseshit."

"Suit yourself." She gave a shrug, then stepped back into the corridor, closing the door softly behind her.

CHAPTER 30

If my life depended on it, I would never have admitted to Frima how long it took me to get out of the dress.

Every swear word I had ever learned left my lips as I fought with the heavy velvet fabric and the intricate gold lace. The tiny hooks in the collar were enough to put me into a rage, and when I realized I then had to remove the dozens of pins from my hair, I had had enough.

I picked up the glass of fae wine, and downed it.

I had precious few hours left to sleep and my head, heart and body were burning with too much energy to have any chance of rest.

I believed that Prince would not take advantage of me while I slept. And I believed that Frima had been right about my room being safe. I was under the Prince's protection, and the door was locked with magic I assumed only his warriors knew how to get through.

If I had a shot at uninterrupted sleep, I was going to take it.

It didn't take long for a pleasant fuzziness to wash over my senses, and within ten minutes, I found myself enjoying the meditative act of combing my fingers through my hair, looking for pins.

When I was sure I had them all, I put on the long shift and clambered into the unnecessarily large bed.

My mind blessedly slow, I fell asleep in seconds.

I was laying on a stone table, the surface cool and smooth beneath my bare skin. Completely bare skin, I realized. I was wearing nothing at all.

I pushed myself up onto my elbows and blinked around, frowning when I realized where I was.

I was inside the trunk of *Yggdrasil*.

The soft trickling sound of the water and the bright, warm glow of light was glorious after days in the gloom of the Shadow Court, and a smile played around my lips.

"You should smile more, *gildi*."

My eyes snapped to the end of the table. Prince Mazrith was standing there, and I sucked in a breath.

He was wearing no shirt, and he was magnificent.

His body was a thing of glory, hard and muscular, and dusted with dark hair. His sculpted abs and wide, powerful shoulders covered in tattoos of runes. Huge arms, corded with muscle, hung at his sides, his hands clenched into fists. His hair was loose, falling around his shoulders, and his bright eyes glittered as he stared down at me.

All of me.

I squeezed my thighs together, feeling my whole body grow hot.

He made a growling noise deep in his chest.

"Do you know what *gildi* means?"

I shook my head.

"It means feast. You, my betrothed, are my feast."

And he truly looked like he wanted to devour me, eyes roving over every inch of skin.

I scooted back on the stone table.

"This is a dream." The words left my own lips, and I paused, considering them.

This was a dream. A surreal awareness descended over me as I blinked around, first at my revered surroundings, then at the half-naked fae prince before me.

"This is a dream." I said it louder, accepting it.

Mazrith's smile turned wicked. "Then there's no harm in letting me do as I like with you."

I shook my head. "I won't let you touch me."

His eyes raked over my naked body and he made that growling noise deep in his throat again. "You will."

"No."

His eyes left my breasts, and found mine. "If I swear not to touch you will you let yourself enjoy this dream of yours?"

I narrowed my eyes.

Fae couldn't get into dreams.

Could they?

No, I told myself. I had been warned that fae wine would make me dream about sex, and here I was, dreaming about sex.

This was only in my head.

Curiosity crept over me as I relaxed. "What could you do without touching me?"

He raised one hand slowly, and his staff appeared in it.

Definitely a dream. Fae couldn't make staffs appear out of nowhere.

A sliver of shadow flowed from the tip of the staff, and Mazrith ran a tongue over his full lips, eyes darkening.

"What... what are you going to do?"

"I'm not going to lay a finger on you," he replied. The shadow flowed toward me, whispering over my clenched together knees. "But I'm going to make you beg me to."

"I won't beg."

"You will."

The shadow pressed against my knees, and I gasped as it touched my skin. It was so cold. It flowed over my bare legs and hips, sending goosebumps prickling over my skin, and I shivered.

"I won't."

"You won't just beg for my touch," he growled. A moan escaped my lips as the shadow crept up my stomach, its coldness making my nipples stand up hard. It flowed around them, sending shivers straight to my center.

"I won't beg you for anything," I hissed, locking my eyes on his. They were alive with desire. With need.

"You will beg me for this." At his words, his trousers disappeared.

Freya help me, everything else around me disappeared. I couldn't take my eyes from what was between his legs.

He was so big. Huge and hard, and standing up his stomach, glistening and thick.

"No, I won't." My voice was breathy and weak. The shadow circled around my nipples, sending tingles of pleasure through my body. Mazrith groaned, and grasped his cock with his hand, moving it up and down slowly.

Heat flooded my core and I bit down hard on my lip.

It's a dream. It's a dream.

The shadow flowed down my stomach, reaching my knees. Slowly, it eased them apart.

It's a dream.

I relented, letting my knees fall and exposing myself to the Prince.

His grip tightened as his eyes fell on me.

"You're beautiful," he growled. "And you want me."

My wetness must have shown, and I whimpered as the shadow crept closer and closer to my core, swirling trails of icy pleasure up my inner thighs.

"I will not beg," I ground out, still unable to take my

eyes from his hand, slowly and deliberately stroking his huge cock.

The shadow pressed to my wetness, and I cried out, my hips jerking.

It was so cold, and I was so hot.

It moved again, flowing around my most sensitive areas, exploring. My eyes closed as pleasure rushed through me. I groaned as the shadow danced over my clit, sending sparks of searing sensation rippling through me.

"You will beg me to fill you."

My breathing deepened and the cold grew more intense, so cool against my burning core.

I rocked my hips, aching for the touch to be firmer.

"You will beg me to make you scream."

My body was on fire. I was so hot, so wet. The cold of the shadow was the only thing that could quench the heat flooding my body.

"One day," Mazrith growled. "One day you will plead for my cock. You will beg for me to fuck you. And I will take you, and you will be mine."

Every word he spoke seemed to fuel the pleasure the shadow was wrapping me in, the pressure in my core growing. I moaned and pressed my hips forward, pressing myself into the shadow.

"Look at me," Mazrith growled. I opened my eyes, seeing his hand moving hard and fast around his massive cock, and the burning desire in his face.

I couldn't tear my eyes away from him. The shadow

danced over my clit, the pleasure building to a crescendo inside of me. I couldn't speak, barely able to breathe.

It was too much. The heat, the pleasure, the sight of him. It was all too much.

With a cry, I exploded.

Every muscle in my body tensed and froze, my hips jerking forward again and again. I felt as if I were floating, my vision white and my body tingling. Sensation flowed through me, from my toes to my fingertips, everything alight with intense pleasure. Mazrith groaned, his hand pumping hard around his cock, then he leaned back, eyes closing. His cock jerked, a thick pearl of his seed spilling over his hand, and then another and another.

I swallowed, my body aching and my core still throbbing with pleasure, and my eyes glued to the sight before me.

A loud banging crashed through my hazy pleasure.

"What the..."

Mazrith's eyes found mine. "Time to wake up, *gildi*."

CHAPTER 31

I sat up straight in my bed, heart pounding, face burning, and body alight.

"Reyna, get dressed," called Frima's voice through the door.

I didn't reply, staring around the room in confusion, sensation pulsing through my core.

It was a dream. Just a dream. I patted my hands over my body, checking. My shift was still on, and I was in bed alone.

It had just been a dream.

My dream.

I drew in a breath. I had no idea my brain was capable of something so... so *filthy*. Did I have a thing about his shadows? Where the fates had that come from?

His hungry eyes, his huge cock, his sultry promises all flooded back to me, and desire washed through my body.

I didn't want to beg anyone for anything. But when

he'd spoken to me like that... I had never wanted anything more.

The door clicked, then swung open. I squeaked in surprise, gripping my sheets and yanking them right up to my chin defensively. Frima stepped into the room. She was dressed in her fighting leathers, and her lips quirked into a wry smile as she looked between me and the empty wine glass.

"Get washed and dressed. Brynja isn't bringing your breakfast to your room, I'm taking you downstairs instead."

"To the Queen?" I croaked.

"No." Her smile softened. "With Lhoris and Kara in the thrall quarters. It's a gesture of goodwill from the Prince."

I blinked at her. "Really?"

"Really. I'll wait outside."

As soon as she was gone, I scrambled out of bed, trying to get reality to flood the surreal dream from my system.

The Prince was letting me see my friends. And I wanted nothing more. Except maybe a cold bath.

I glared at the empty wineglass as I made my way quickly into the bathing chamber. I washed in cool water, trying to douse the heat the dream had caused. Slowly, as the fuzz from sleep ebbed away completely, the sensations pulsing through my body lessened. I forced myself to picture the Prince, dressed. Dressed in lots of clothes; shirts and cloaks and furs.

He had kidnapped me. Threatened to kill my friends.

I did not want to see him naked. I did not want his shadows on my body. I did not want to beg him for anything.

He was only being nice to me today because he needed me to work hard for him, and he wasn't stupid. The best way to get me to co-operate was through my friends. He knew that.

But that didn't lessen how pleased I was that I would be able to see them, and I needed to concentrate on them.

I exited the bathing chamber in a hurry. I had clean shirts and trousers in my shouldersack and pushed my hand under the pillow to retrieve it from its hiding place. But there was nothing there. I pulled everything off the bed, searching frantically, but it was gone.

I let out a growl of anger. The staff in that bag was worth an absolute fortune. And in the hands of a gold-fae, it was a powerful weapon. Could someone have known I smuggled it in?

I kicked the bed post. That had been my only source of money. The ace up my sleeve. And now it was gone.

Cursing under my breath, I stamped to the wardrobe to pull out the clothes I had arrived in. I was surprised when I yanked them out that they smelled of chalky powder and lemons. They had been cleaned, I guessed by Brynja.

The maid had access to my room, I thought, pulling on my trousers. Who else did? All of the warriors, and the Prince. I tried to remember when I'd last checked the bag was there. Before I went to the statues with the Prince was the last time I remembered seeing it. But he had been with me the whole time I had been outside my room, and so had Frima.

Svangrior had been walking away from my room when we returned, but I had seen nothing on his person that looked like my bag, or a place he could have been hiding it.

Maybe the thief took it during the ball?

Dressed, I picked up the warded headband from the desk and did my best to twirl my hair around it, so that it was away from my face. I stuck Voror's feather into the side of it, less artfully than Brynja managed, but it would have to do.

With one last scowl at my reflection, I turned to bang on the door. Frima opened it.

"Why do you look so pissed? I thought you'd be happy to see your friends," she said as I stomped out of the room.

I considered telling her about the bag. But I still didn't trust her, and I had no reason to be this mad about clothes being stolen. Telling her would raise suspicion about what was actually in there.

Whoever took it must have known the gold staff was in there, I thought. Who would have stolen clothes?

"I'm just tired," I said as we began to walk down the gloomy corridor.

"Dreams keep you up?"

My face heated as memories of the dream coiled through me, making my muscles clench. "No. I don't know what all fuss is about with that wine."

"Liar," she chuckled.

"Can, erm, fae get into dreams?" I asked, as casually as I could.

She laughed. "Not unless they're high fae. Who have been extinct since the gods left. Why? Did you get a visit from a fae in your sleep?" Her eyes sparkled.

I glared at her, then at the seemingly endless maroon walls. "I fucking hate this color," I snapped.

Frima looked at the walls. "You prefer gleaming white and gold?"

"I have no idea what I prefer."

She didn't answer.

We walked in silence the rest of the way, and this time I did pay close attention to the route. I'd found my way to the thrall quarters once on my own, but knowing the quickest way couldn't hurt.

The long table in the middle of the large room was deserted, and Frima hurried me to the barred room I knew Lhoris and Kara were in. "You have twenty minutes, before everyone returns. Keep your voices down."

She unlocked the door and shoved me in.

Kara was on me in seconds, wrapping me in a hug. I hugged her back, savoring the moment I hadn't thought I'd be given.

"How are you doing?" I asked her when she released

me. Lhoris was sitting on the floor of the room amid a swath of loaded plates. Cheeses, breads, cold meats, and a tray of fruits I mostly didn't recognize surrounded him. He smiled up at me, huge beard twitching.

"We're good," Kara said. "How are you?" Concern filled her big eyes.

"Better than I thought I would be."

"Sit. Eat. Tell us," said Lhoris.

After peering out of the bars to make sure Frima wasn't hanging around to listen, I did as he said, taking as much food as I could fit on a plate. Today would be a long day, I knew.

"I assume since we weren't punished for the other night, that you took the brunt," he said quietly, eyes scanning my bare forearms for evidence of my punishment.

I shook my head. "Svangrior didn't tell the Prince. Or punish me."

Lhoris cocked his head. "Why not?"

"He, erm, gave me an incentive to not try again that he thought would work better."

The big man nodded knowingly, glanced at Kara, and took a bite of cheese. She looked at me excitedly. "Did that owl really talk to us? Lhoris said he still can't really believe it," she said in a rush.

I smiled at her. "Yup. He really did. He's called Voror, and he has a pretty high opinion of himself."

Her mouth dropped open. "I told you so!" she said, turning to Lhoris.

He gave her an acknowledging nod, then turned to

me. "Sounds like you have learned a lot since we last spoke. Tell us."

Indecision sparked in me. Did I risk telling them about the statues? I didn't know enough about them yet to have anything useful to share, so it wasn't worth the risk, I decided.

"The Prince warded this headband so that the Queen can't get into my head, then told me there is a place where he thinks there might be gold," I said, deliberately vague in my half-truth.

"What place?"

I shook my head. "I don't know." An outright lie, but one to protect them. They were not warded against the Queen, after all.

"And the owl?"

"Sent by a fae woman to assist me. He doesn't know who she is, and nor do I." Lhoris paused shoveling food into his mouth.

"Sent to help you?" he repeated.

I nodded. There was no way I was going to tell them that she'd also said the fate of *Yggdrasil* depended on me. Just thinking about it made my head swim, and I forced the thought out.

"I always knew you were special," Lhoris muttered.

"What?"

"Your hair. Your complete lack of past. Reyna, you are being sought."

The words reinforced my own realization, and to my surprise, I drew comfort from that. "Yes."

"I'm not sure you can run from this."

"I know. But that doesn't mean I'm giving up." I looked at Kara, willing my sincerity to sound in my words. "When I know more, we'll have leverage. We'll get out, it just might not be through running."

"Although if an opportunity arises..." Lhoris said ruefully.

"Oh, don't worry. I'm not getting complacent."

He smiled. "What else has happened?"

Between mouthfuls of food, and as succinctly as I could, I told them about the trip to the workshop, and the ball. Everything except the finer details of my inter-actions with the Prince. *And the dream.*

"Please tell me you don't believe he may not be the monster everyone says he is?" Lhoris asked, voice hard.

"Of course not." *Even though part of me is starting to want to.*

Forcing memories of the dream out, I focused on devouring what was left on my plate. "Someone stole my bag."

Lhoris' face darkened. "The staff is gone?"

I nodded. "They must have known it was there."

"They can't have. Perhaps they went through your things and got lucky." He let out an angry breath as Kara spoke, tapping her finger against her jaw thoughtfully.

"So somebody gave you a key to get out of your room and then opened the bear cage, and somebody stole your bag. Do you think they're the same person?"

I stared at her. "Opened the bear cage?"

She nodded, fine hair falling around her cheeks. "Yes. Don't you remember hearing the mechanism?"

"Well yeah, but I never thought..." I played the events back in my mind, and realized she could be right. Someone could have deliberately opened the cage. "You think they gave me the key to lure us into danger?" Frima's words about the whole escape attempt being suicidal came back to me. If whoever gave me the key had the same thought then perhaps I didn't have the secret ally I thought I did.

"Maybe. Are there people here who would want you gone?"

I snorted. "The Queen, for sure. Maybe Svangrior. He seems to hate me with a little more passion than is necessary."

"What about the female fae?" Lhoris asked.

I shook my head. "She's playing a different game. Trying to get me to trust her, I think."

"None of them can be trusted," he barked.

"I know." I swallowed hard, then turned to Kara. "So, what have you two been doing?"

"They give us tasks to do in here, but we're not allowed out," Kara said.

"They can't risk anyone seeing your rune-marks."

"But everybody knows you're here if the Queen threw a ball to announce it," she said. "Why do we have to be kept secret?"

"Because any slave or fae courtier here might decide to use one of us to get on the good side of the Queen," Lhoris said gently. "We are safer in here, although I admit it is becoming stifling."

I glanced around at the windowless walls, feeling

guilty about both my trip out on the horse to Tait's village, and the fresh air at the ball.

"Hopefully you won't be in here too much longer," I said, though I had nothing to follow the statement with.

"Indeed," said Lhoris. "Find out everything you can about what the Prince wants with you. Keep your eyes and ears open at all times. And whatever you do, do not fall under their spell." His eyes bored into mine as I nodded. He had no idea just how strong that spell could be.

CHAPTER 32

All too soon, Frima's soft voice called through the bars it he door. "Let's go, Reyna."

I got to my feet, hugging first Kara, then Lhoris.

"I'll see you soon."

"Be safe," said Lhoris.

"Die trying," I answered him with a smile.

As Frima and I walked along the quiet corridors I felt surprisingly ready for whatever was coming next. I had a full belly, my friends were safe, and I wanted to know more the statues. *And possibly more about myself.*

Thinking about the Prince caused an uneasy feeling to invade my determination though, Lhoris' hard eyes a warning in my mind.

My mentor was right.

Of course I couldn't trust Prince Mazrith. It was just a

fae spell that made me react so viscerally to him. And the fact that he had not been cruel to any of us yet was because he needed my help, and he needed me strong and healthy.

I needed to remember that whenever that accursed dream floated into my head. Fucking fae wine.

"Did you enjoy seeing your friends?" Frima asked me, pulling me from my thoughts.

"They are being treated well," I replied. I wasn't going to let her draw me in.

"As you were told they would be."

"Hmm."

"You're not going to grace me with your gratitude?"

"You said I had Mazrith to thank."

She tipped one shoulder up. "True. I'll have to find another way to earn your precious manners."

Annoyance pricked at me. "You expect thralls to be polite to you, but it means nothing. At least when I say it, it matters."

She chuckled. "You sound like Maz."

I glared at her as we rounded the corner into the raven room corridor.

"Get your tools, Maz will be along for you in a while," she said when we got to my door, pushing it open.

"You're dying to ask me where he's taking me, aren't you?" I said as I stepped into my room.

She kept her face even, but I saw her eyes twitch. "He'll tell me when he needs me to know." She slammed the door shut harder than she needed to, and I wondered if baiting her was a good idea.

Sighing, I made my way to the bathing chamber, kicking the door open.

I froze.

A snake as big as my arm slithered over the edge of the tub. And it was no shadow snake. It was as bright blue as the water snake had been, with rings of white circling its thick body. It hissed as it writhed forward, flicking out a forked tongue.

Instinct kicked in, and I slammed the door shut again, scooting backward. Keeping my eyes fixed on the bathing chamber door, I kept stepping backward until I reached the main door to my room.

Banging on it hard, I yelled.

"Anyone there? There's a snake in my room, and he doesn't look friendly!"

There was no answer.

A soft thud sounded against the bathing chamber door, and then it creaked open. Foot after foot of blue scales emerged as the snake slithered out, and my pulse began to race. How fucking long was this thing?

I banged harder on the door. "Hello? Anyone out there?"

The snake's eyes were fixed on me, and they were as black as night. I groped to my side for anything that I could use to defend myself, but found nothing. The torches in the wall sconces were too high for me to reach, and the snake was between me and the burning embers in the fireplace.

I glanced at the bed and saw the heavy tool roll. There were scalpels in there, and a small hammer. I didn't know how much damage they could do to a snake that size, or how well I would be able to defend myself with them, but they would be better than nothing.

Taking a slow step sideways, I kept my eyes glued to the snake. It stopped moving, instead lifting its head off the ground and swinging it from side to side, tasting the air.

I stepped again, reaching out toward my bed and the tool roll. The snake darted forward, so fast it was a bright blue blur. I dove onto the bed, rolling as I hit the mattress.

But I'd been too slow.

I felt a searing hot pain in my foot, and then I was tugged backward hard. I scrabbled at the blankets as I was dragged back across the bed, trying to grab at the tool roll and failing to grasp it. The pain in my foot was agony, white hot and spreading fast up my shin.

I hit the stone floor with a bang and swiveled around, trying to get free of the snake's grip. But its fangs were deep in my foot, and every time I tugged the pain became unbearable.

I turned wildly, struggling into a sitting position, looking for anything I could use as a weapon. The pain in my foot was so intense it was making my eyes stream, and my head fog.

The snake's body swung around, tail crashing into my ribs.

I cried out and doubled over before the tail came down on me again, this time across my shoulders.

A bang in the distance was followed by the muffled sound of someone calling my name.

"Reyna?"

"Help!" I screamed. The door handle rattled, but the door stayed shut.

The snake's tail whipped around again, catching me hard enough to knock me onto my side. The movement shifted my leg, and with it my foot. I felt the flesh tear, and everything in my vision swam as pain like nothing I'd ever felt tore through me.

I saw another flash of bright blue as the tail came toward my face, and barely got my arms up in time to block it. The banging on the door faded to nothing, replaced by the sound of my own blood pounding in my ears. Black dots swam before me, and the pain began to ebb away.

I was getting sleepy.

A new noise drifted through to me. A male voice? My eyelids drooped, and delicious warmth washed over me.

A spasm of pain cut through my cozy haze, and in my blurry vision I saw something bright blue rising through the air, surrounded by dark smoke. Or was it shadows?

My body jolted, and then I was rising too. Someone was carrying me, I thought dimly.

The sleepiness came and went for what could have been minutes, or hours.

I knew on occasion that something hurt, and wished the warmth would return. But whenever it did, a dark-haired figure with purple streaks slapped me on my cheeks and returned me to the uncomfortable place.

I tried to speak a few times, but no sound came out. It didn't matter. All I wanted to say was that I was tired. That they should leave me alone.

A number of times I was given something bitter to drink. Swallowing didn't really work, and hands on my shoulders moved me around roughly until I could feel the liquid rolling down my throat, like the water in the root-rivers, rushing along their wooden channels.

I began to dream about rivers. Endless rivers, flowing and swirling around a mighty tree. But then the rivers changed. They were red. Red with blood. And rising from the water, everywhere I looked, were the Starved Ones.

CHAPTER 33

I woke with a start, my hand clutching my chest and my brow covered in sweat. I drew in great gulps of air, looking for the monsters, but seeing only warm walls and a burning fire.

I blinked around, trying to work through the fog in my head and the dull throbbing in my foot.

There had been a snake in my room, and it had bitten me. Someone had come in and picked me up? And this room... It looked a little like mine. I was in a bed, but it was much bigger than the one in my room. All the blankets were black and silver, and the furniture was all oversized.

There was a door on my left, half open, and through it I could see a sitting room, with an armchair I thought I recognized.

The walls weren't maroon. The significance of that filtered through the bleariness slowly. I had only been in one other room that didn't have the blood-colored walls.

I was in the Prince's rooms.

Had he come and dealt with the snake?

Movement caught my eye through the door, along with the sound of angry footsteps, and I forced my tired eyes to focus.

"Tell me where you were." It was the Prince's voice, and he sounded furious.

A human man backed into view, both his hands held up and fear on his bearded face. "Your highness, I was tasked with guarding the floor, not the raven rooms. I didn't know—"

Shadows preceded the masked Prince stepping into view, swirling and diving at the terrified man. "Tell me who did this to her." His voice was the hissing of a thousand snakes, laced with power and rage.

"Your Highness, I saw nobody," the man whimpered.

"Lies."

"Nobody came through the stairs I was posted at, I swear it." He hunched his shoulders as the shadows closed in around him. Crying sounded in the distance, high-pitched and fearful.

"Tell me who did this to her."

The man began to lift off the floor, the shadows pouring under his clothes and around his face.

He let out a wail and tried to beat his arms. "I can see him," he gasped.

"See who?"

"My father. He has the axe..." The man's eyes were wide with fear, and a sob burst from his chest. "Make him stop!" He screamed. He tried to shield his face with his arms, but the shadows pinned them to his sides.

"You will watch that scene, over and over, until you tell me what I want to know."

"There was nobody. Please. Please."

The Prince raised his staff, and the man screamed.

"If you will not tell me, I will take it myself."

The shadows zoomed to the man's head, rushing into his open mouth.

My breath caught, horror overwhelming me.

For an eternally long second, the man just hovered, black shade flowing into his body. Then he crumpled to the ground, the shadows flowing back to the Prince's staff.

"Take him," the Prince barked. Frima stepped into view, picking the man up by his armpits. As she straightened, she glanced my way. I stared back, numbly.

"She's awake, Maz," she said quietly, then disappeared.

When the Prince strode into the room, my body reacted instinctively. I scooted backward, tucking myself into a tight ball, covering my head with my arms.

Fear like I'd never known was coursing through my veins, making my limbs shake and my brain too slow.

"You have been poisoned."

I moved my arm a fraction. The shining black skull stared down at me. I tucked my head behind my arms again.

261

"Stay out of my head. Please, please, please. Stay out of my head." The words issued from my lips in a stumbling unbidden stream.

Silence answered me. A long, painfully fearful silence. When I finally moved my arms again to look, he was gone.

~

I stayed huddled in a ball, the after-effects of experiencing such fear making me feel as sick as the growing pain in my foot.

I had seen cruel bullying, vicious beatings, and painful grief in my time with the fae, none of which had produced such an extreme reaction.

The only time I remembered ever feeling so scared was after I had the first vision.

I tried to make myself think about the snake, about the fact that someone had apparently tried to kill me.

But my exhausted mind kept tracking back to the shadows filling the man's mouth, and the Prince's shining black skull mask. Cold and hard and utterly emotionless.

I tried to get angry, tried to let my default emotion to take over, give me strength. But I was too tired. Too confused.

I knew who the Prince of the Shadow Court was. The rumors were true.

. . .

I tried to stay awake, fear making me believe that sleeping wasn't safe. But exhaustion dragged me under, no amount of adrenaline able to contend with it.

When I next awoke, Brynja was leaning over me, concern filling her bright eyes. "My lady? Do you need anything?"

"Water," I mumbled thickly when swallowing made my throat stick.

She passed me a full glass of cool water. "The Prince said you would need lots of water."

"Thank you." I gulped down as much as I could manage. My foot hurt less, though my head pounded.

The crippling fear that had swallowed me whole had mercifully released me, my limbs working again, my mind clearer.

Images of the guard and the shadows, and the Prince's mask, churned around in my head though, and I took a deep breath and closed my eyes.

He had seen me weak. Physically terrified. A coward, backed up and begging.

"Are we in his rooms?" I asked Brynja without opening my eyes.

"Yes, my lady. He's in the sitting room."

My heart stuttered in my chest.

I couldn't be scared of him.

If I was scared of him, he would win. I would never be able to take my chance if it arose.

Die trying.

I wasn't going to give up.

I had to face my fears.

ELIZA RAINE

I opened my eyes. "Could you ask him to come in, please?"

She nodded nervously and scurried out of the room. The Prince strode in a second later.

My stomach flipped over at the sight of his face. No mask. And no staff either, I realized as I scanned his empty hands. "Why did you do that to him?" I forced the words out, relieved when they came.

"He was lying to me. And I needed the truth."

"Why was he talking about his father?"

"This is not what is important."

"Tell me."

He stared into my eyes, and I made myself hold the gaze, even though my insides trembled. "I made him see his worst memory. When I realized that wasn't enough to make him tell me the truth, I took it from him by force."

"What did his father do with the axe?"

"Reyna, that is not important," he snapped, and I flinched. When he spoke again, his tone was calmer. "What is important is that he was lying. Rangvald came up the stairs he was guarding."

"You think Rangvald put the snake in my room?"

"It is possible. The only other person seen in that wing was Svangrior."

"Why?"

"I don't know. And he is under my stepmother's protection, so it will not be easy to find out."

"Why can't you just send your shadows into his

264

head?" I couldn't help the wobble in my voice, and I clenched my teeth as my cheeks heated.

"He is warded against me. As I warded you against the Queen."

"You..." I trailed off trying to find the words I needed. Shame and anger were making me hot, and I couldn't deny the trickle of fear that had started up on seeing him.

Shade danced across his bright eyes, and he lifted a large hand to his jaw, rubbing his fingers across the stubble. "You were poisoned. By the snake bite."

My foot was covered by blankets, and I shifted it awkwardly. "Did you... Was it you who... saved me?" I ended reluctantly.

"I killed the snake and administered the antidote, yes. You will be ok, but your foot will hurt." More shade crossed his eyes. "The venom may have caused other adverse effects."

I frowned. "What do you mean?"

"Heightened emotions. Strange dreams. Out-of-character reactions."

His words hung in the air and I stared at him. Was he saying I got so scared of him because of the snake bite?

Hope flared through the shame. Could it be true?

The thought of him inside my head terrified me, for sure. But if he was willing to see my reaction as the result of poison over cowardice...

"I need you to visit the shrine."

"But someone just tried to kill me with a snake. And my foot hurts."

His huge body tensed, and his eyes narrowed. "I will find out who tried to kill you. In the meantime, I need you working on the statues."

A tiny gold rune sparked to life on his jaw, before rising into the air and fading away. He took a hurried step backward. "I will send in your maid. Get washed and dressed, and we must return to the shrine." I didn't have time to open my mouth before he had gone.

I stared mutely at the empty space he had just filled.

The Prince of the Shadow Court had secrets.

Any misconception I had started to build of him, any false notions of integrity, or even compassion, had been irrevocably dispelled on seeing what he had done to the guard.

My bound betrothed was the the monster the world said he was. Which meant I was in a war.

An all-powerful fae with a plan, versus a lowly human with an unknown past and future.

But the folk of Yggdrasil were born for war.

I would do whatever I could to win.

CHAPTER 34

It was a few long minutes before I got up the courage to inspect the state of my foot, and when I pulled back the blankets, my stomach dropped. There was no way it would heal quickly.

I had two puncture marks on both the top and bottom of my foot. The ones on the outer side of my foot had torn, presumably when I'd tried to pull my foot free. The edges of the cuts were black, as though they had burned, and the skin around the wounds was a sickly grey-green.

I tentatively poked at one of the holes. It didn't hurt as much as I thought it would. The black scabbing over the cuts felt solid as rock, and after a moment more probing, I was confident that they wouldn't bleed if I moved too much or put boots on.

Slowly, I set both feet on the carpeted floor. An uncomfortable throb was all that met me, so I stood.

There was a slightly painful pressure on the outside

of my foot, but not enough to stop me walking. Carefully, I took a few steps, looking for the bathing chamber.

"Oh, my lady!" Brynja's voice startled me, and I whipped around, losing my balance and reaching out for a bed post. The maid hurried toward me. "I can't believe what happened. Are you okay?" She looked down at my green foot, and recoiled. "Oh, that looks..."

"I'm fine," I told her.

"Really? What can I do for you? I have your working clothes here." She pointed out into the sitting room.

"A bath would be good," I told her. Cold sweat had covered my body most of the hours I had been in the bed, either from the snake venom or the overwhelming fear the cursed Prince had caused.

The unexpected flash of rage when I thought about it comforted me. I was moving past fear, into anger. And anger was far more useful.

Brynja helped me bathe without getting my foot wet, and then helped me dress. The headband had stayed on my tangled hair during the struggle with the snake, but Voror's feather had not survived the incident.

I wanted to see the imperious owl, but I didn't know when or how. He might have seen who stole my bag, and put the snake in my room.

"Brynja, did you see anyone near my room before the snake?"

"It was a snake?" Her pink cheeks turned pale.

"Yes."

She shook her head as she tidied my hair, shaking her shoulders like she had something unpleasant on her. "I can't abide snakes, my lady. I would have clean passed out from fear."

"I think I did pass out, but from poison. I've never been that scared of snakes," I said, then glanced down at my now carefully booted foot. "Although I suppose I might be now."

"What scares you then, my lady?"

"Being trapped."

She gave me a knowing look in the mirror. "I think most thralls fear that," she said quietly.

I gave her a small smile. "Not my friend Kara. She was born a slave, and her biggest fear is never getting to read a book again."

"I've been talking with Kara," Brynja smiled at me.

"Really?"

"Yes. I'm the only one who knows who they really are, your friends," she said proudly. "I take them their meals and small jobs to do, like darning and horseshoes. The big man, Lhoris, he's handy with a hammer."

It made sense that if Brynja already knew about me, then she would be looking after Kara and Lhoris.

I reached up and squeezed her hand without thinking. "Thank you."

She smiled. "I'll try and smuggle Kara a book. She's sweet."

"She is. This is no place for her."

"Was it any better in the Gold Court palace?" Brynja asked.

269

The question wasn't rhetorical; it sounded like she was genuinely asking. "Yes. We had our workshop, and Kara and I were safe from male attention, being rune-marked."

Brynja stiffened slightly. "Not many thralls have that kind of protection."

"I'm sorry. For anything that has happened to you."

She shrugged again. "Not your fault, my lady. Right, that's you all fixed up." She stepped back and I got to my feet a little stiffly.

"Thank you. You know, I really appreciate everything you've done for me."

Her cheeks pinked. "You're welcome, my lady."

There was a knock at the door, and I heard the Prince's voice. "Are you ready?"

The narrow passage through the rock to the shrine was no less disconcerting than the first time. The Prince and I had barely exchanged words, an uncomfortable friction humming in the air between us.

When the little boat emerged into the cavern, I could see the wrist rising from the water, holding the statues aloft over the cascading waterfall below.

We moved straight to it and I took a breath as I clambered out of the boat and onto the stone.

"Do you need help?"

I glared up at him. "No."

He glanced at my injured foot, then began to walk slowly along the stone arm.

I fixed my sight on him and walked, making an effort to breathe evenly and ignore the discomfort from my foot. I wasn't afraid of heights specifically, but I would have challenged anyone walking over the chasm not to take extra care.

Anyone except the Prince.

A new set of worries flowed through me as I reached the palm of the hand, and the statues.

The gold-vision would descend if there really was gold under the stone, and I was sure there was. And I had no doubt the dark visions would follow. How would I deal with them in front of the Prince?

I would lie to him, of course. Tell him something else was happening, and that it happened to all *gold-givers* after they worked.

The idea of him knowing about the visions filled me with a dread I couldn't explain, and it made me wonder if it was connected to my fear of him getting into my head. I wasn't sure what it was I feared so much about others knowing, just that I had a deep-rooted certainty that it was a secret I had to keep as my own.

He watched me as he set the tool roll that he had carried down in front of the gold-fae statue. "Begin your work."

I narrowed my eyes at him, before moving to the statue's staff.

Taking great care, I began to work, painstakingly removing the stone from the gold. The gold-vision flicked in and out as I brushed my skin against the metal underneath, but it never descended fully, taking me into the engulfing trance.

The Prince's deep voice made me pause. "I must leave."

"What?" I turned to him. "I'll be trapped here. I can't make the boat move back to the passage."

"You are a prisoner in my palace. You are trapped anywhere you are."

I glared at him, but was secretly glad he was leaving. If I could complete my work whilst he wasn't there, I would be alone when the dark visions came.

"Don't leave me down here to die," I snapped, not wanting to arouse him suspicion by looking like I'd had a change of heart.

His eyes flashed. "I will be back shortly," he said, then spun on his heel.

CHAPTER 35

I swallowed down the apprehension that rose in me when I thought of being stranded in the cavern, stuck hanging over the chasm below.

I forced myself to concentrate on the statue before me, keen to get as much as I could done before he returned.

A soft hoot from above made me jump in surprise and look up. There was a fluttering of wings, and a white owl swooped out of the darkness. A surprising rush of relief hit me at not being alone.

The owl soared down to the statues, dropping a single feather down to me before perching on one of the figures with no face. "*Heimskr.*"

"Please call me Reyna."

"No. This place has power."

"I know. How did you get here?"

"I followed you. It was not easy, given how much

stone I had to travel through, but my superior skills were able to seek you out."

"Well done," I told him. "Did you see who put the snake in my room?"

The owl froze. "Snake?"

"Yes. The massive blue snake left in my room to kill me."

"I saw no snakes. When I returned to the palace you were not in your room. I assumed you were indulging in human affairs with the fae male whose bed you were in when I located you."

"I was poisoned. By a snakebite. That's why I was in his rooms."

"Snakes are vile creatures," Voror said, flicking his wings, and shifting his weight.

I tilted my head, trying not to smile. "Are you afraid of them?"

He ruffled his feathers indignantly. "I am afraid of nothing!"

"Of course you're not. What about this place?" I spread my hand out, gesturing at the statues. "Do you recognize anything?"

He moved his head slowly, taking in each statue. "These are the fae of the five Courts. I do not know who these two are, but,"—he paused, lifting off then resettling on the statue that was much shorter than the rest—"this, I believe may be a dwarf."

My eyebrows lifted. "Dwarfs? I thought they were a myth?"

He clicked his beak. "They were as real as the gods and the high fae were once," he said.

I looked back at the statues. "Could one of the other two be a high-fae?"

"Possibly. What is your task here?"

I pointed to the inscription on the circle in the middle of the palm. "That says I have some sort of key. And the gold-fae statue has gold inside its staff. But something's not right. The gold is bent."

"You are repairing it?"

"I'm removing the stone first, and then yes."

"Do you know how to repair it?"

"The gold runes will tell me what to do."

The owl tilted his head again. "Do you think it wise to help the Prince of the Shadow Court?"

I bit my lip as I considered. I had no more reason to trust Voror than anyone else. But I did. "Whatever this place is, I am involved. This was inscribed centuries before I was even born. If I am truly the only one who can uncover whatever it is hidden here, then perhaps the leverage that affords me can take me further than running."

Voror blinked. "Where is it you wish to go?"

"I want to be free. I don't want to hide. I don't want to move through *Yggdrasil* knowing I will be killed or enslaved for who I was born as."

"You believe you can ransom whatever you might uncover for your freedom?"

"I think it is as likely to work as trying to escape."

"And what if the knowledge you hand over to the

Shadow Court in exchange for your freedom spells a worse fate?"

"Like what?"

"War. The loss of the rest of your kind's freedom." He ruffled his feathers again in what I thought was a shrug. "Cataclysmic disaster."

"I see you're an optimist," I muttered. He was right, though. I had no idea what kind of power I was dealing with here, or what it might do in the wrong hands.

"I am not an optimist. I am wise."

"You can't be both?"

"Absolutely not."

"I disagree."

"Well, you're not as clever as me."

I scowled at him. "So you keep telling me. What, oh wise one, would you do in my position?"

"I would find out more about the power here. Then decide what value it has."

I put my hand on my hip. "And how can I find out more about the power without repairing the staff?"

Voror was silent a moment. "You can't. Continue your work, irritating human."

I shook my head as I moved back to the gold-fae statue. "You know, if enough people keep calling me that, I may develop a complex."

Hours passed, and I was able to uncover the top part of the statue without causing any damage to the gold. I could still only see one bent feather, and a little thrill came over me when it was finally time to fix it. Picking up the finest scalpel I had been given, I laid my hands firmly on the gold feathers and embraced the gold-vision. If I could work fast enough, then hopefully the Prince would still be gone when the dark visions came. It would be easier to lie about them to Voror; the owl couldn't get into my head.

The runes began to float from the metal, and I slipped quickly under their spell. I was vaguely aware that they were different from the usual runes I saw. I couldn't quite pinpoint how; it was something to do with the angle of the lines, and the sharpness of the points. Something subtle. Not wrong, or overwhelming. Just different.

I worked diligently on straightening out the feather, placing my scalpel carefully and rubbing my fingertips over the gold exactly as the runes instructed me to do. When I finished, I crouched, dropping my tools and allowing the gold-vision to lift.

"I find myself enjoying watching you work," said Voror, his voice making me start slightly.

"Wow. A compliment."

"It would appear you are not adept at taking them."

"I haven't had much practice. Look, Voror, there's a... *thing* that happens after the rune-marked work. I need intense, uninterrupted rest for a short while." I moved onto my backside as I spoke, laying the palms of my hands on the cool stone and making sure I was sitting in the middle of the hand-shaped platform. I would lose my real sight any moment, and I had no inclination to be anywhere close to the edge when that happened.

"Understood. Do you wish me to leave?"

"Yes. Please."

"Very well." I heard the fluttering of his wings and closed my eyes.

The first wave hit me. Darkness. And strong sense of unease, bordering on fear, but too intangible to solidify.

I took a deep breath, rubbing my hands on the stone, trying to ground myself.

But when the second wave came, my breath caught in my throat.

It was different.

There was no screeching laugh. A woman was crying instead. And the flashes of red illuminating shapes in the darkness were flashes of silver.

The vision faded as quickly as it always did, and gooseflesh rose on my arms. In my whole life, the visions had never changed. The third always started with an ear-splitting scream. I'd stopped rubbing my hands over the stone, instead balling them into tense, sweaty fists.

Never would I have believed that I would be hoping for that scream.

It didn't come.

A wail sounded in my ears, long and raw, and filled with sadness. Two figures came in hazy view, a man crouched over a woman laid on her back. The smell of blood always came next, but instead, I became aware of the smell of flowers. Lilies.

The vision cleared, and I opened my eyes, panic crawling up my throat.

I hated the visions of the Starved Ones, but to see something different? It had thrown me almost more than anything else that had happened to me.

Would there be a fourth?

Darkness descended, and I instinctively wrapped my arms around myself, fear taking me in its clutches.

A face moved into view. Not the Starved One I usually saw. It was a woman, face pale and haggard. "My son." I gasped at the words. Never had I heard words before. "If they find out what you really are, they will end you."

A male voice answered, distorted and grief-stricken. "I have no magic without you. Please. Don't leave me."

"My death will give you enough for five years. But you must find the mist-staff by your thirtieth birthday."

"No! No, mother, you can't!" The woman's face faded from view and then eyes shone out of the patchy gloom left behind.

The vision cleared as I groped for the stone beneath me.

Those eyes.

They had been gold, not gray, but there was no doubt in my mind who they belonged to.

The Prince.

I moved unsteadily, suddenly needing to be anywhere but trapped underground. I needed space, air, a chance to breathe.

I stumbled to my feet and remembered I was on a platform over a lethal drop.

Some of my confused, claustrophobic panic gave way to sense.

I had to wait for the Prince. Where was he?

Could it really have been him in that vision?

Turning to the waterfall, I half expected to see his form striding along the wrist toward me.

What I did not expect was the hooded figure standing just a foot away.

CHAPTER 36

I cried out in surprise, but the sound was lost as the figure shoved me, hard.

Without even a few seconds to register what was happening, I found myself tumbling to the stone.

Instinct took over, and I scrabbled to my knees, stopping myself from rolling. But my assailant was too quick. A boot landed hard in my stomach, and with enough force I was forced over again.

Arms flailing, I reached for a statue as it rolled into my view. I wrapped my arms around the base of it as the boot connected again with my shoulder. My torso and legs swung out, and for a heart-stopping second, I felt nothing but clear air beneath my body.

I summoned my strength, pulling myself back up using the statue. Pain burst through me as the boot began to kick at my arms and hands. I swung my body, ignoring the pain as best I could as I tried to swing my legs back up to the platform.

There was a loud screech, and the kicks to my arms stopped abruptly. A hiss reached me as I finally managed to get my foot back onto the stone hand.

Heaving myself up, I saw the white wings of Voror as he pecked wildly at the black-cloaked figure.

"Pull off the hood!" I yelled at the owl as I shakily crawled further onto the platform. Voror dove again for the figure, but they swiped at him with something metal and shining. He let out a squawk as it connected, then veered off out of sight.

"Voror!" I jumped to my feet, but pain lanced through the wound in my foot, making me stumble. I caught myself on the nearest statue, stumbling again as my vision turned gold.

Shit.

I'd grabbed the exposed gold staff.

As I let go, I saw a flash of metal and leaped to the side just in time to avoid the knife the figure had swung at me. I got a glimpse of a black mask covering the face under the hood.

"Who are you?"

They didn't answer but kicked out at me again. They connected with my hip, and I staggered backward. I grabbed for the statue, everything turning gold as I gripped the staff top. But the gold was too soft to take the force of my weight hitting it, and the part I'd exposed broke away in my hand. My stomach lurched as everything seemed to move in slow motion, momentum carrying me backward, straight off the edge of the stone hand.

I didn't scream as I fell.

The sound of water crashing filled my ears as my hair whipped up in front of my face. A weird calm came over me, and I felt strangely lucky I could the see the spiky ceiling of the cavern, instead of the certain death I was plummeting toward. It was all gold. I was still clutching the staff top, and it somehow seemed fitting that I would die with the gold-vision.

Something slammed into my side, and I spun in the air.

A cry of shock escaped my lips, but my breath was too hard to catch, I was falling so fast. A dark pool flashed into view beneath me as I turned in thin air, then a blur of white crashed into me again.

Voror?

What was he doing?

Again he hit me, and when I spun, I saw the water below me again, only this time, a patch of it was darker. And closer. Nausea churned in my gut as I kept spinning, and I squeezed my eyes closed.

Any second now, I was going to hit the surface of the water. The impact was sure to kill me. And if it didn't, the rocks below would.

Voror slammed into the side of me again, just a second before I hit.

Only, I didn't hit water. All the breath left my body as my back connected with something soft. Time froze as I desperately tried to get air into my lungs, then water began to seep through my clothes.

I was sinking.

Air finally made its way down my throat and I flung my arms out, trying to clear the daze.

I was on a bed of weeds. A thick coating of moss floating on the surface, that had cushioned my fall.

I kicked my legs, the water freezing. I was seeing everything in gold. Shoving the piece of staff into my pocket I pushed myself into the water, fearful of becoming tangled up in the weeds and dragged down.

I looked around dazedly for Voror.

He'd pushed me so that I'd fall on the weeds. The owl had saved my life.

I spotted him, hovering over a dark crack in the cavern wall, on the opposite side of the rocks the water-fall was crashing down onto. The noise was deafening, and I felt like I was living some sort of surreal dream. Every part of me ached, and each kick of my legs drained more energy from my body.

The current was moving me toward the crack though, and I let it, trying to conserve what I could. I glanced up at the stone hand, but it was so high it was just a dark speck against the cavern ceiling.

Who had just tried to kill me? How had they even known about the cavern? Not only known about it, but known to drink the water, had a way to open the secret door, and cross the pool to the wrist without being carried over the edge.

Voror hooted as I reached the crevice in the rock. I didn't have his feather, so I couldn't hear him speak, but he ducked into the dark crack. Assuming I was meant to follow, I swam after him.

The current intensified, and a shriek of surprise left me as I was carried along much faster than I expected. The passage curved and twisted through the rock, barely wide enough for me. My limbs caught constantly on the rough rock, scratching and tearing my skin.

All my attention was on keeping my head above the water as I was tossed along the tunnel for what seemed like an age. I was running on pure adrenaline, fatigue threatening to drag me under. Every time I thought my body might give up, I heard a hoot from above, and redoubled my efforts, kicking my aching legs and flailing my scratched and bleeding arms.

When my body was just about ready to give up the fight, the passageway bent sharply. I was thrust against the cold, sharp rock wall, and then I saw light. The tunnel through the rock was opening.

First relief, then fear, washed over me as I was ejected from the mountain into a huge river below. The fall was not as far as I thought, but it was enough that my whole body was submerged. I opened my eyes in shock as I was engulfed by the cold water, and they immediately began to sting. I dredged up all the strength I had left, forcing my way back to the surface.

Hooting reached me the second my head was clear of the water, and I blinked, looking for the owl. He was the only fleck of white in my blurry, gloomy surroundings, and I swam half-blind toward him. Blessedly soon, my feet kicked something below the surface.

The ground.

I stumbled, my foot throbbing and my knees scraping the stony surface as I practically clawed my way onto dry land.

Collapsing on what I thought was sand, I rolled onto my back, panting.

My limbs felt like they weighed as much as a horse. A white feather drifted down beside me, and I made myself lift my hand enough to grasp it.

"Voror."

"Reyna. Are you well?"

"No. No, I'm not well. But thanks to you, I'm alive."

"It is my task to assist the copper-haired *gold-giver*," he said proudly.

"Top assisting," I breathed.

"Do you know who just tried to kill you?"

"No. Do you?"

"No."

"Do you know where we are?"

"No. I can smell and hear predators though."

I was outside the palace.

The realization forced a tiny bit of energy through my body, and I made myself sit up.

I was on a small shore on the side of a wide river. Gnarled trees rose on each side of the waterway, the twilight sky twinkling with stars overhead providing the only light. The mountain loomed behind me, and I had to crane my neck to see the palace at the top, glittering towns dotting the ridges on the way back down.

If the shrine was under the palace, in the middle of the mountain, then I must have fallen all the way to the bottom and then the channel had carried me out. I was a long, long way from where I had started.

A distant howl made me turn to look behind me. Dense trees, fortunately not as twisted or creepy looking as the ones we had ridden through the day before, loomed.

"What kind of predators can you smell?" I asked Voror.

"Wolves. Bears. Some I can't identify."

It wasn't just predators I needed to be wary of outside the palace. If any human of the Shadow Court found a rune-marked, they would kill them instantly.

"Any humans?"

"I don't believe so. You are bleeding though, and that will attract carnivores attentions."

I looked over my arms, and wished I'd been wearing something sturdier than cotton. The sleeves of my shirt were shredded and torn and stained with blood from dozens of small scratches. My thick woolen trousers had fared better, only a few tears around the knees, and my leather boots and body-wrap had held up well.

"I need somewhere safe to clean up and rest. Any ideas?"

"I would suggest, up a tree."

"That's because you are a bird."

"It is also because wolves can't climb trees. There is a pack nearby, and I think they are coming closer."

CHAPTER 37

Resting in a tree turned out to be more comfortable than I imagined it would. Voror had found one that was easily big enough to accommodate me, a criss-crossing of heavy branches forming a sturdy platform well off the ground.

"Can bears get up here?" I asked, as I peered down at the ground. Inside the canopy of the tree, it was much darker, little of the twilight sky's light getting through.

"Some could, yes."

I looked at him, perched on a branch a few feet from where I was wedged securely. "Are we safe here?"

"I will alert you, should such a bear come."

"Thanks." There was a rustling noise, and my body tensed.

"A mouse."

"How do you know?"

"My eyesight is excellent. As are my other senses. All superior to yours."

"Oh. Good."

The owl rolled his head slowly. "Except your magical sense."

"You mean the gold-vision?" I suddenly became aware of the weight of the staff top in my pocket.

"Yes. What happens to you after you work with the gold?"

I swallowed. "I get fatigued."

"And you prefer to be alone for this fatigue?" he sounded doubtful.

"Yes. I do not like to display weakness to others."

"Ah," he said, mollified. "I understand."

I closed my eyes, trying to remember the details of the vision I'd had just before the attacker had given me a lot more to worry about.

Could that have been the Prince? And if so, had that been his mother?

Or, had the figure, emerging from the gloom, been him coming to kill whoever the woman and her son were?

If they find out what you really are, they will end you.

I couldn't help the certainty I felt that she was talking about the Prince. I knew he was keeping a secret. Why the fates else would gold runes keep drifting from his skin?

She had mentioned his thirtieth birthday, and a mist-staff. I had never heard of a mist-staff. But could that be what the Prince was so desperate to use me to find?

Waves of tiredness washed over me, making it hard to think clearly.

"What will you do now?" Voror said in my head. "You had decided not to run, but here you are. Free."

The same thought had been flying around my head from the second I'd stopped swimming for my life.

I was outside the palace. But everything had changed.

"I'm not free."

"You are not bound." My eyes flicked open at the word.

"That's exactly what I am. Bound. To the Prince."

Voror blinked at me. "You mean metaphorically?"

"Magically. I am his bound betrothed." I let out a long breath. "I am bound to my friends, too. I made a promise that they wouldn't be hurt. I can't keep that promise from here."

"You intend to return to the palace?"

"If I run, then I'll be found. The Prince has made that clear. My friends will be killed. And even if I could live with that—which I can't—and evade the Prince—which I doubt—your mysterious fae woman will probably show up," I said with a shrug. "I can't run from this."

The owl moved his head slowly. "I agree. You have a fate to fulfill. Fate cannot be outrun."

I closed my eyes. "So, here's a sentence I never thought I'd say. I'm going to get some sleep, and once I'm strong enough, we'll make our way back to the Shadow Court palace."

. . .

With Voror keeping watch and confidence in the branches holding my weight, I was asleep in seconds. Exhaustion made sure of that.

A sharp feeling in my arm jolted me from my deep sleep.

"Reyna." Voror's mental voice didn't sound right. My body was stiff and sore, but my mind was alert quickly.

"What's wrong?" It was dark, even the low light coming from the sky seeming dimmer, and I could only just make out the white shape of the owl.

"Something is coming."

"Wolves? The bears who can climb trees?"

"No. Something much worse." He sounded... scared.

My stomach knotted. "What?"

"I hope I am wrong, but the stench.... I fear it is unmistakeable."

My skin felt cold. "Stench?" A cracking sound in the distance was followed by a long howl.

"Reyna, I don't know whether you should stay here, hidden, or whether you should run."

My eyes were adjusting to the gloom, and I could see his wings fluttering. There was another howl, which turned into a yelp, then cut off completely. Icy fear flowed through me.

"Voror, please. What is coming?"

"The Starved Ones."

Blood rushed in my ears, my skin prickling with fear. "No. They can't be."

"Stay here." He beat his wings, rising up out the tree.

"Voror!" I hissed, but he was gone. I rammed his

feather into the waistband of my trousers, then rolled as quietly as I could into a better position, where I could see the forest floor below.

He must be mistaken. Nobody had seen a Starved One in years.

Other than the one you saw on the root-river, I thought, swallowing hard.

And the ones you see in your visions.

Rustling from above made me suck in a breath, then Voror drifted down through the branches.

"False alarm?" I whispered hopefully.

"You will not be able to outrun them."

Numbness washed over me. "It's really them?"

"Yes. More than I have ever seen together at one time." The owl sounded as serious and as scared as I felt.

"Odin help us. Maybe they'll go right on by us, if we don't make a sound."

"They will be able to scent your wounds."

"What?" I stared through the trees branches at the forest below, my heart beating hard in my chest. Movement caught my eye, and it skipped a beat altogether.

Something dark was moving jerkily between the trees.

The humanoid form was just a black silhouette, moving as though it were dragging one leg, a pronounced hunch to its right shoulder.

A wail sounded through the trees, and every muscle in my body stiffened.

More figures appeared amongst the trees, all moving awkwardly.

Out of nowhere, a rotten hand burst through the branches below me, and I kicked out. My breath was coming so short that I was getting light-headed. Fear so intense it was almost blinding was engulfing my senses.

Cold, slimy fingers closed around my ankle, and tugged hard.

"Voror!" I screamed, as I was ripped from the branch. I reached out, trying to grab hold of anything but the grip was too strong. Tree bark scratched at my limbs as I was pulled down, bouncing off more solid branches.

Wailing filled my ears as I struggled, and the smell was overpowering. Rotten meat and putrid sweetness. The grip on my leg loosened, and my feet touched the ground, my view still obscured by dark-leaved branches.

I ran.

I couldn't see properly in the gloom, and all I knew was that I was surrounded by the creatures, an eye here, a gaping jaw there, a sewn together arm or a skeletal hole coming into view before fading away as I ran.

They kept up with me. Grabbing at my clothes, pulling at my shoulders, yanking me back every time I moved forward. It was a game. They had let me run. They were hunting me, playing with their food.

Thick trees surrounded us, and every time I slipped from their grasp, I hit a trunk. My footing caught in a tangle of roots and terror washed over me as I went down onto my knees.

They had me.

I tried. I tried to get back to my feet. To keep running. But they were over me in an instant, blocking out the light. Red maws, rotten hands, exposed teeth clicking in excitement. I was going to become one of them.

They would eat my flesh, tear me apart. Sew me back together with what was left of their other victims.

And I would become one of them.

Freezing cold washed over me, and I knew it was the end. Fear wouldn't let me stay awake for this. I prayed for unconsciousness as pain tore through my shoulder-blade.

But it didn't come. The cold intensified, and then the wailing got louder.

"Run!"

Numb fear warred with reality as the bellowed word slammed into me. The hands and teeth pulling at me all vanished. Light seeped back through the throng of monsters.

"Reyna, do you hear me? Run!"

The Prince.

As one, the Starved Ones surrounding me turned, hissing and gnashing their teeth.

An explosion of black snakes erupted from the ground, coiling themselves around the Starved Ones. I staggered to my feet, turning blindly. White caught my eye in the dark, and I pushed through the thrashing monsters, running for what I was praying was Voror.

I reached the owl, slamming into the tree he landed on, gripping it as I gasped for breath.

"He is strong. But I don't know if he is strong enough."

I turned, feeling sick, adrenaline pounding through me.

Prince Mazrith was standing in the clearing, and the sight of him made my ragged breath catch.

He was fucking *godly*.

His eyes were blazing ice-white in the darkness, his staff glowing with silver as shadows poured from it. They solidified as more snakes, wrapping themselves around the hideous creatures and dragging them to the ground. One of them launched itself at him, and a slither of shade shot out of the staff. When the stream of shadow reached the creature it entered the gaping hole in its chest. The Starved One froze, then exploded.

I gripped the tree trunk harder, pressing myself into it. "He looks strong enough to me," I whispered.

A voice sang out into the darkness, and the Prince went still.

"Gold Ones, Dark Ones, Starved Ones," the female voice sang. "Too bright, too blind, too hungry."

The shadow snakes pinning the Starved Ones to the ground began to break apart, and the Prince snarled. More shade poured from his staff, and the hideous creatures began to make a new noise, a snickering, laughing screech.

My knees felt weak when the voice spoke again, and I saw a figure in the distance, through the thick trees. A large figure, as big as the Prince. "Are you hungry, your highness?"

"Leave my realm!" The Prince roared.

"You don't know what it's like, do you? To eat, and eat, and eat, and never feel the bliss it must be to be sated." She gave a small laugh. "Only, maybe you do. What do you yearn for, your highness? Flesh? Bone? The screams of your enemies?"

The figure had stopped twenty feet from the mass of Starved Ones, most of whom had regained their footing and were staring at me or the Prince. Fear had my feet rooted to the spot. "Leave my realm, now," hissed Prince Mazrith.

"Give us the girl."

My stomach flipped, and gooseflesh tightened my skin.

"You will never have her."

"You can have her back. When we are done with her."

"You will never have her," Mazrith growled. Shadows billowed out around him, and then swamped the crowd of Starved Ones.

Suddenly, it was too dark to see anything. I could hear wails and screams and the roars of the Prince, but I could see nothing.

"Up! Get up!" It was Voror, and I groped blindly behind me for the tree trunk, grateful for any kind of direction. My mind was a swimming mass of fear and confusion. All I knew for sure was that I couldn't outrun them.

A new roar sounded as I pulled myself desperately up the tree.

I'd heard that roar before.

I risked a look over my shoulder and saw a bear, six feet at the shoulder, crashing through the trees towards the figure. Silver bands glowed around its shoulders and limbs, just like Jarl.

A colossal boom sounded, and then light exploded through the forest, right as the bear smashed into the figure. I turned my head, pressing myself to the tree trunk and shielding my eyes from the painfully bright light. A keening wail started, exactly like the sound I heard in my visions, and then cut off abruptly. A crunching sound was followed by a human-sounding moan.

I turned around slowly.

The Prince was standing in what was now a clearing. It looked like a fire had blitzed through the trees, the exploded parts of twenty or more Starved Ones littering the scorched ground around him.

The massive bear was behind him in the distance, ripping something off a body.

I moved my terrified eyes back to the Prince. His blazing ice-blue eyes bore into mine. "She is coming," he said.

"Who?"

"The Queen. Run."

Then he collapsed to the ground.

THANKS FOR READING!

Thank you so much for reading Court of Ravens and Ruin, I hope you enjoyed it! And I am a little bit sorry about the cliff :)

The story continues in the next book, Court of Greed and Gold.

You can also get exclusive first looks at artwork and story ideas, plus free short stories and audiobooks if you sign up to my newsletter at elizaraine.com.